THE BEEF JERKY GANG

By

DANIEL KENNEY

To my wife Teresa and to our children Anna, Isaac, Jude, Brendan, Daniel, Rachel, Fulton, and Joshua

ACKNOWLEDGEMENTS

I want to thank my wife and children for putting up with me through the writing of my books. You know that writing makes me happy and I love you for it.

To my critique group partners. Alison, Amy, Emily, Jenny, Nancy and Sarah. You have helped me become the writer I am today. Which means, if I'm terrible, then it's all your fault. But truly, you laughed and cared about Peter, Plumpy, Gary, and Izmir before anybody else. You helped me find their story. I am in your debt.

To Johnny for helping me with my opening chapters, Mrs. Heithoff's students, who read my manuscript and gave me their feedback.

To Brian Martone for his amazing cover illustration, and to Jerry Dorris for pulling everything together in a fantastic cover design.

To Cheryl Perez for her mad skills designing the e-book and print book.

To David Gatewood, a far, far better editor than I deserve, than I will ever deserve.

And finally, to Caroline Beery, my seventh and eighth grade English teacher. After I completely bombed on my *"Why Dick Clark Is An American Hero"* speech at the beginning of seventh grade, you watched as I became deathly afraid of speaking in public. And yet, you haunted me, finally pushing me a year and a half later to join speech and debate. Michelle and I took first place that year and you taught me a valuable lesson: face your fears, work hard, and good things will happen. Thank you!

TABLE OF CONTENTS

CHAPTER ONE

THE FALCON

A microscopic bit of meat dangled from the end of my fork.

"You only got one?" Plumpy asked while taking a cautious bite of the day's special, *Twisted Wind Salad.*

I surveyed the bowl again, just to be sure. A pile of green leaves, something orange that was not in fact an orange, and a white slimy substance without even a hint of taste.

But no, not another piece of meat.

I shook my head in disgust. "Okay Gary, you're next."

The small kid directly across from me jumped as if I'd spooked him, which was weird, since he'd counted after me every day for the past two years.

"Well," his voice squeaked, "I've got four normal-size pieces, one that I'd call half a piece, and a little bit of grizzle."

Plumpy frowned and held up his finger. "Grizzle is another way of saying the word 'gray.' What you mean is gristle, the cartilage attached to meat."

I rarely understood what Plumpy was talking about. This time was no exception.

"Not bad Gary, not bad at all," I said, shocked that I'd once again gotten so little meat. "Okay Plumps, how about you?"

Plumpy already had his brown bits lined up and was inspecting them through a small magnifying glass he always carried. He looked like a scientist studying mineral samples.

"Five normal pieces and an extra piece of meat skin." He snapped his head up. "But no gristle."

I weighed the decision in my head. "I'd call that a tie. Gristle's worth skin and a half piece, right?" I looked around for agreement, and the guys all nodded.

"That leaves you, Izmir," I said, almost afraid of what was about to happen. Izmir leaned back, cracked his knuckles and grunted. Oh no.

Izmir was Turkish, and we really didn't know what that meant. We knew he looked a little different than the rest of us—and a lot like the rest of his family. He was also basically crazy, but we didn't blame his family for that. That part was just Izmir.

He cleared his throat, rubbed his hands together, and showed off each piece individually.

"That makes five normal pieces, two shards of skin, and last but not yeast..." Plumpy and I exchanged the usual look—the one we shared whenever Izmir screwed up a common saying. "A broken bone."

"You're lying," Gary squeaked as he jumped out of his seat.

Izmir proudly displayed the bone for all to see, and sure enough, it looked real.

"Okay," I said, waving my hand in defeat. "Izmir's got it. You're on quite a roll. What's that—three days in a row?"

"Four days, Peter, four days in a row." Izmir smiled as he started to gnaw on the bone.

Crazy or not, I envied that guy.

"Peter, how is it that you are so unlucky?" Izmir asked, the little bone sticking out of the corner of his mouth.

"Yeah," Plumpy added. "You've been getting stiffed on your meat count for the last couple weeks."

The meat we were talking about was best described as mystery meat. None of us guys knew what it was or where it came from, but we were certain it wasn't a piece of iceberg lettuce, and thus we didn't care. The few bites of meat in our school lunch salad were all that most of us ever got, and we treasured every last morsel.

And Plumpy was right. Lately I *had* been getting stiffed.

"Did you guys get the newest book yet?" Izmir asked, still working over his leg bone like it was the single tastiest thing in the world.

"*Search for the Perfect Skirt?*" Plumpy asked.

Izmir nodded, and suddenly his face looked like he was in great pain.

I was about to give the guys my usual lecture about why they should never actually read the books when I heard heavy footsteps behind me, followed by that familiar hoarse voice.

"Excuse me, boys." I turned and looked up at The Falcon, our lunch room prefect and psycho gym teacher. The Falcon was at least six feet tall. She had blond hair that was short on the sides like a boy, but poofy on top, and she wore the collar up on her way-too-small *Finley Junior High* polo shirts. She once told us that wearing small shirts allowed her to take us on a magical adventure to the gun show. Then she did a quick double biceps pose to show us those guns.

The Falcon grabbed the end of the table and leaned forward, looking like she might just snap the thing in two. "Doesn't look like you've eaten too much of your salad today. Something wrong?"

We had learned from experience not to mess with The Falcon. One time, after some of the boys on the cheerleading squad left behind their trash, she'd grabbed their table and flipped it over like a dinner plate.

Plumpy shoveled a forkful of salad in his mouth. I did the same.

"Nope, nothing wrong at all, Ms. Falcon," I mumbled through a mouth of leafy lettuce.

The Falcon examined her left bicep as if it was the most fascinating thing in the world, then turned her head back toward me.

"Peter, I noticed that you and your friends signed up for the Quilting Team this year. Any reason you didn't think about Synchronized Swimming instead?"

Well yes, I thought, watching the jaw muscles in The Falcon's face twitch as she worked over a wad of minty green gum. Quilting is easy and requires no physical exertion, while synchronized swimming is pure pain wrapped in a shiny pink swimsuit.

"We, um, don't…*want* to do synchronized swimming?" I said it more like a question.

The Falcon looked at me like I'd just won Finley's annual Dumbest Boy in School contest, then shook her head and surveyed the other guys. Each one had his head down, chewing furiously.

"Well Peter, that won't do. That won't do at all." She blew a green mint bubble and popped it in my face. I knew what was coming.

Although there was no rule that you had to go out for spring sports, The Falcon used her unique skills of torture—er, *persuasion*—to ensure participation. She took personal responsibility for the health and fitness of every Finley student and expected to field a competitive sports program. As she was fond of telling us, fat kids and lousy teams were "Falcon failures."

"Nope, Peter, synchronized swimming is where you need to be. I've seen you all swim, and for boys, you're not terrible."

I took a big swig from my bottle of spring water. "But we just *really* like quilting, Ms. Falcon. Can't get enough of it, right guys?" The guys nodded along with me. I hoped The Falcon would get bored and move along.

She didn't. Instead she danced her knuckles against the table and studied me up and down. Then she made a face, like whatever she'd seen in me was unacceptable.

"I'm not so sure you can afford to go a whole term without exercise."

Huh? "Thank you for your concern, Ms. Falcon, but I think I'll manage."

The Falcon did not like to be refused. She bored her eyes into me like I was a set of dumbbells she was about to dominate.

"Truth is, quilting will have to wait," she said firmly. "I need four boys to field a full synchronized swimming team, and I need the best."

"And *we're* the best?" asked Plumpy.

"Like I said, you're not terrible—and that'll have to do. Those pasta-loving goons from Noodles Junior High have beaten us fifteen years in a row." She punched her own hand so hard I thought it would split in two. "But I'm determined to change the synchronized swimming fortunes of our school, and I'm counting on you boys to help." She spread her hands above her and got a faraway look in her eyes. "I can just picture those judges from the Correction handing me the trophy now. *Finley Junior High, 2075 Regional Champions.*"

Stay strong, Peter. I swigged some water and took a deep breath.

"Thanks for the offer, Ms. Falcon, but…we pass."

She cocked her head. "Do we have a problem here?"

"Just that me and the guys have big plans for our quilts this spring. But thank you anyway."

I shoved another hunk of lettuce in my mouth. The Falcon cracked her knuckles and then bent over me.

"So we *do* have a problem. You know, Peter, as minister of health and fitness for the school, it's within my power to make you come before school, make you stay after school, do whatever it takes to fix your little problem." She leaned down close enough that I could smell the Old Spice venting from her neck. She started whispering in a really creepy voice. "Just as long as we do, in fact, *fix the problem.*"

The Falcon flared her nostrils and showed her teeth, kind of like her old dog Vicious would do before trying to eat a kid's pants.

I swallowed hard, and a mouthful of salad doesn't go down smooth.

"So you boys will join the team?" she said at last.

Plumpy and Izmir both shook their heads at me. Gary sniffled from under the table. I tried to get the word "no" to come out of my mouth, but then a hand clamped onto the back of my neck and started to squeeze.

"*You're* going to be on the team, Peter, am I right?"

I pictured The Falcon squeezing so hard that my head popped off like a cork out of champagne bottle. A gurgling sound came from my throat and a word slipped out. A tiny word.

"Yes."

She whacked me on the back and salad shot out of my mouth. It hit Izmir in the face. "Excellent, Peter. Knew I could count on you and the rest of the guys." She glanced around the table and the guys nodded helplessly.

"Practice starts tomorrow after school. And remember, if you don't have the money for a one-piece, the school has a fund to help you out." She rubbed her hands together. "And finish your salad— you'll need the extra nourishment. In case you hadn't heard, synchro is the toughest thing you quilt-loving softies will ever do."

The Falcon strutted away and kissed both biceps. It was her signature move—how she demonstrated dominance. She had just marked her territory.

Apparently I was her territory.

Gary was still trembling, Plumpy stared at the ceiling, and Izmir was shaking his head at me, eyes full of rage.

"Peter, you folded like a cheap boot," he said, wiping salad shrapnel off his face.

"Cheap suit, Izmir. I folded like a cheap *suit*. And wait a second, no, I didn't. I mean, what was I supposed to do?"

Gary's eyes were wet. "Why, Peter? Why?"

"Don't start with me, Gary. You can't even form complete sentences when The Falcon's around."

Plumpy continued to stare at the ceiling while twiddling his fingers. "One moment we were minding our business, counting mystery meat bits, and the next moment we're committed to dancing around in a big bathtub wearing one-pieces." Plumpy sat upright and leaned toward me. "Why did she call it a one-piece? Aren't all boy swimsuits one piece?"

I sighed. "Don't think she was talking about boy swimsuits."

It took a few moments, but then a wave of recognition came over Plumpy's face and he looked like he might also cry.

I don't know how long we sat there—maybe a minute, maybe it was ten. I just know we were all in a daze.

When the bell finally rang, we threw away our half-eaten salads and carried our still-hungry stomachs out of the Polka Dot Bistro. I opened my locker to get books for the afternoon, and a note fell to the floor.

Uh-oh. Notes were never good. I'd received my share of notes through the years, mostly death threats from Jessica Hale. I wondered if this might have something to do with synchro. I unfolded the note, and the first thing that jumped out was the handwriting. Not bubbly, not pretty, in fact not good in any way. This was the unmistakably terrible writing of... a boy.

I scanned the hallway. Boys didn't write notes. At least, no boy I'd ever met. I studied the squiggly block letters until I could make out the words. I read them over three times until I was sure I knew what the note was saying.

A strange message. A very strange message.

ARE YOU READY FOR THE TRUTH?

CHAPTER TWO

SQUISHY

No doubt about it, synchronized swimming was going to be bad. Real bad. And parts of me that I'd rather not mention clenched just thinking about the level of pain in store for me when I was scheduled to jump into the pool in twenty-four hours. Even so, something about that weird note was bothering me even more. What boy would do something like that? And what truth was he talking about?

I was brought back to the land of the living by a pounding on my desk. Mrs. Dorney hovered over me, smiling with her enormous lipstick-painted mouth.

"Don't you agree, Peter?"

"Yes?" I said in the least convincing voice ever.

"You have no idea what I was saying, do you?"

I froze.

"Then how about next time you enter my class prepared to listen, all righty? Peter, I was telling the class how I think *Ophelia*

Smart Gets Real will in the very near future be considered a literary classic. Yes indeed, a literary classic."

At that point, my brain once again switched to the off position. I had heard this speech before. To Mrs. Dorney, *every* book we read was a literary classic... or was destined to be one soon. As usual, I hadn't actually bothered to read the book—I'd just glanced at the chapter headings and skimmed the rest. And to be fair, even the term "skimmed" was being generous. I had learned long ago that these fine works of literature all had the same ingredients. Lonely girl. New school. A struggle to fit in. Lots of feelings. Shopping was usually involved. And a horse. The great authors must have had a formula. When in doubt, add horse. Or shopping. And in a *real* emergency, shop for a horse.

Dorney wrapped up her lecture and asked the class if we noticed anything about her outfit. This was a daily exercise with Dorney, because she always had something new she wanted to show off. Sometimes it was a new hairdo, like the "stuck her head in a blender and add color" style she'd been wearing lately. But usually it was a new shirt or skirt she'd purchased for herself in the "Li'l Miss" section of the clothing store. When no one answered, she leaned so far forward I thought she would tip over—which would have been awesome. But she didn't tip. Instead, bright gold monstrosities swung from her ears.

"Is it your new earrings?" one of the girls in the front row asked. I think it was Marcie. She was always answering questions, because of course she actually read those "literary classics."

"Oh, aren't you a dear? You noticed. New *hoop* earrings to be precise, and I do—" she hesitated, a smile broadening across her face. "I do *hoop* you like them." Dorney snort-laughed so hard I thought she might swallow her own face. When she was finally able to calm herself down, she sat, took out her pen, and began to tap it against her metal desk. We all knew what was coming.

Time for questions.

Although I hated everything about school, I hated talks about why I wasn't prepared for school even worse. Usually, that excruciating topic came up with my mother. I called those conversations the "not up to par, with air quotes" talks, because Mom would tell me about a teacher calling her at work to inform her "Peter was 'not up to par' today," and she would always do giant air quotes. Every time. It was like she got paid by the number of air quotes she could work into our talks.

But now it was Mrs. Dorney's turn to call me to task. At least she didn't use air quotes, but she seemed to enjoy calling on me to prove my level of unpreparedness—and that was partially my own fault. I may have brought unnecessary attention to myself in the past by making the... you know... occasional smart aleck remark. And for better or worse, the woman didn't seem to have the ability to appreciate real humor. Or *my* humor.

After scanning the room for potential victims, Dorney served up her question. "I need someone to explain how she or he identifies with Ophelia?"

Squeals erupted from around the classroom, and I looked around, a bit startled. Every single girl had her hand up, leaning forward excitedly and just *dying* to answer this question. As for the boys? Most had slumped in their seats, books hiding the panic on their faces, while a few pretended to look for pencils under their desks. One boy openly wept. Still another, the tallest and skinniest boy in our class, was sleeping, though nobody but me could tell.

The tall kid was Plumpy, and he was my best friend. Better known to his parents as Leonard, Plumpy had perfected the art of sleeping with his eyes open... and I do mean *perfected*. My own dad was pretty good at this technique, but Plumps had taken it to a whole new level. He could sleep, hold a pen in his hand, and *not* drop it. Dropping a pen was, of course, a dead giveaway that you were sleeping. Plumpy's trick—and I was the only one who knew it—was double-sided tape. The man was a genius.

Dorney scanned the room again, drinking in the excitement of a room full of girls practically begging to answer her question. Each and every girl could have probably lectured the class for thirty minutes on the book. So, naturally, Dorney called on me.

"Ah, Peter Mills. Peter, Peter, Peter. I would simply *love* to hear your take on our Ophelia. How do you identify with her?"

Of course. First synchronized swimming, then a weirdo leaves me a note, and now Dorney calls on me for questions. Chapter headings, don't fail me now. I carefully cleared my throat and took a deep breath. "Well Mrs. Dorney—"

"Up up up, Peter," Mrs. Dorney said, lifting her hands like she was conducting an orchestra. Wonderful, the privilege of standing for the class. I could hear a combination of snickers by the girls and sighs of relief from the boys.

"Well, of course you've got Ophelia here," I said as I tapped on the book, hoping some gem of understanding might magically transfer into my fingertip. "And she is... you know...alone." I hesitated. The girls were staring and licking their lips, sensing I was ripe for the kill.

"Go on."

"Poor, poor Ophelia. She's really, really alone, Mrs. Dorney."

"I believe you've said that," Dorney said, narrowing her eyes.

"At her grandparents... in the summer. And there's this big old house... you see... a really, really old house...where she lives with her grandparents. And well, this all happens in the summer."

A strange growling noise came from Dorney's throat. She placed her hands on her hips and stepped toward me.

Not a good sign. She wasn't buying any of this. I was desperate.

"But that's not all," I said.

"I should hope not."

"No, no, no... not by a long shot, Mrs. Dorney. This Ophelia, she's what you call a mighty complicated character." I tapped the book a few more times.

I was basically a trapped animal. Like Dorney and the rest of the girls were up on their haunches, ready to pounce on the weakest member of the herd at any moment, when all of a sudden—*bam*, it hit me. The golden rule of being a boy in a girl's world: When in doubt, act like a loser.

"Well, Mrs. Dorney, Ophelia reminds me of how I sometimes feel in the world."

Her eyes brightened, and she leaned forward, her monstrous hoop earrings swinging back and forth, once again looking like she might tip. "Okay, Peter, elaborate."

Mrs. Dorney, like every other girl, loved it when you pointed out just how pathetic boys really were. "It's just that sometimes, the world seems like nothing but a big scary place to me. Ophelia had that big scary house and I have this big scary world. And you know what, Mrs. Dorney?"

"What, Peter?"

I tried to look feeble.

"We're both alone."

"Oh, bravo, Peter, well done." Dorney gave three loud slow claps and then cocked her head, cupping her hand around her ear. "Do you hear that, class? I think the Feelings Train is coming around the bend." She held her hand in the air and pulled, like a train engineer would. "Chooo, chooo," she yelled. "Jump on Peter, jump on the Feelings Train and ride it wherever it goes."

Oh no, I was on the Feelings Train. I knew from… well, let's just call it prior experience… that fighting the Feelings Train was no good. I needed to hop on and get this over with fast. I let my voice drop, slumped my shoulders, and just went for it.

"When I'm alone in this big scary world, I feel small and useless."

"Like you're hardly worth anything?" Dorney asked.

"Yes, ma'am, Mrs. Dorney. That's it, exactly. Like I'm not worth anything, like, uh, nobody understands me, and like I can never be myself. Like I'll never be able to be myself in this world. This crazy, messed-up world."

Here I threw in a sigh and an eye roll for good measure.

"Like I'll always be stuck in this prison. This stupid world that's unfair with all of its rules, rules that don't let me do what I want to do or be what I want to be. This crazy, stupid, unfair, prison of a world that's completely controlled by all of..."

I caught my breath. Both the girls and the boys of the class stared at me. All I could hear was the screeching of chairs and desks across the tile floor.

Dorney cleared her throat and looked around nervously. "Well Peter, I know I said to get on the Feelings Train... but that was just plain weird. And, might I say, more than a little inappropriate. There's nothing whatsoever wrong with our world. Our world is beautiful. Why don't you point that finger of yours back at yourself and worry about Peter Mills for a change. In fact, speaking of Peter Mills, are you sure you even read *Ophelia*?"

A hand shot up at the front of class, and I didn't even need to look to know who it was. It was Jessica Hale. Beautiful, brilliant, athletic, perfect at everything and meaner than—well, there really was no good comparison. To compare her to pure evil would be an insult to evil. We boys figured that long ago Jessica must have approached the Devil with some kind of a secret deal. Or maybe the Devil approached her—I wasn't really sure who the boss was in that relationship. If girls were at the top of the social pyramid, then Jessica Hale was the pharaoh who watched them build it. When we were feeling kind, my friends and I referred to her as the Ice

Princess. She had been enemy number one for as long as I could remember.

"Of course Peter didn't read it, Mrs. Dorney. He's just trying to fake it just like he always does. I think it's pathetic if you ask me."

Did I mention I hated her? At least I nailed the "pathetic" part.

"An astute observation, Miss Hale. That would explain the weird answer and Peter's total derailment of the Feelings Train. Peter, is Jessica telling the truth?"

"What? Of course not, Mrs. Dorney. How could you even ask such a thing?" Acting pathetic was easy. Acting shocked was a bit harder.

She looked at me skeptically. "Okay, Peter, then here's another question. And please keep in mind that I'd hate to have to call your mother again." She took her pen and tapped it against Jessica's desk. "In what other way do you identify with Ophelia? And I would like it to be a way that is very particular to you?" She looked down at Jessica and winked.

Was she speaking some secret girl language? I didn't have a clue what she was talking about. I mentally recalled the chapter headings again and tapped my book a few more times… but finally, I gave up and shrugged.

Dorney threw her hands up, looking completely exasperated. "Peter, Peter, Peter, maybe Ophelia's *body image problem*?" She over-enunciated the last three words. "How do you identify with that?"

Identify with *what*? Ophelia's body image problem? That settled it: Dorney was obviously speaking secret girl language, because I had no idea what a body image problem was, but I promise you it wasn't in the chapter headings.

She let her gaze drop to my feet, then slowly moved her eyes all the way up to my head, like a caterpillar crawling up a branch.

"You know, Peter: how Ophelia would like to be *thinner*?" Dorney said it like she was doing me a huge favor by giving me this hint. I, of course, still had no clue what she was getting at.

She bent her head low and looked down at me through glasses which were now perched at the end of her long, hooked nose. I prayed they might slip off and provide me en exit out of this.

"Like someone you might know very well. Very, very well." And, with her hand, she patted her belly and then pointed at mine.

Oh my mother. Dorney was talking about me.

As soon as I realized it, I could feel my face growing hot and my palms go sweaty. Dorney was calling me fat. In front of Jessica Hale, in front of Plumpy, in front of everyone.

Jessica laughed. "I see what you're talking about, Mrs. Dorney." She did?

"You know," Jessica continued, "it's not too difficult to be in shape. All it takes is eating the right foods, exercise, and a little discipline."

"Is that how *you* manage to look so fantastic, Miss Hale?" Dorney asked, as if Jessica were the most fabulous creature on earth.

"Honestly? My superior genetics certainly help. With Peter's natural shortcomings there's a limit to how good he can look, but..." She snapped her fingers like she'd just had a great idea. I couldn't wait.

"I bet there's plenty of good diet books in the library. That would be a really fun project for Peter, getting a diet book and trying to lose weight. He could report back to the class. I bet we'd all learn so much from him."

Dorney nodded her head like Jessica had just discovered the cure for a disease. "I like the way you think, Miss Hale. That's the kind of leadership that one day will make you head of the Whitfield Corporation, just like your mother. I'm sure she's very proud of you."

"Oh, she sure is, Mrs. Dorney."

"And class, Jessica has a good point," Dorney said. "Even at your age, some of you kids," she turned and looked right at me, "especially those who are a bit… squishy… can afford to lose some weight."

Squishy?

I don't know if I ever wanted to die nearly as much as I did at that exact moment.

Dorney scribbled on a piece of paper and handed it to me. "Here's a library pass, Peter. Go find yourself a good diet book—in fact, find two or three—then lose that weight and report back to us later this semester."

"Wait… what? Are you serious?"

Dorney folded her arms and breathed in through her nose, looking at me sternly. "Completely." Then she walked back up to the front of the class and patted Jessica on the shoulder.

Jessica gave me The Look. The look I had seen at least a thousand times before in my short yet miserable life. The official

Jessica Hale Look of Triumph that they probably taught her in Ice Princess training. It wasn't enough that Jessica was perfect; she had to find every single opportunity to point out that the rest of us were not. Mostly me.

"Now class, we learned so much today. Literature gives us iconic figures like Henrietta Hairspray and Ophelia Smart so we can climb into their skins and walk a mile in their stiletto heels. Let's allow these beautiful characters to breathe their energy through us each and every day. Oh, and Peter, maybe Ophelia might help you to get a little *real* yourself." She snort-laughed and dangled her pointy finger at my belly, the girls laughing along with her.

And then, a miracle. The bell rang.

"Okay dears, for homework, remember to read the first two chapters of our newest selection, which I might add is also destined to be a literary classic: *Darcey Jones*."

I looked at Jessica, and she narrowed her eyes at me. Then she put her hand to her face and coughed, yelling the word "Squishy!" at the same time.

And like that, a new nickname was born.

A group of girls crowded behind Jessica and followed their evil leader out of class. I could have clubbed myself to death.

Synchronized swimming. Weird note.

And now, squishy.

CHAPTER THREE

BROKEN WORLD

I stared at that library pass until I was the last person in the classroom. Well, except for Plumpy, who, incredibly, was positioned like a statue, eyes open, pen firmly in hand, and yet still asleep. I punched him in the shoulder and he jolted awake.

"Sorry Mrs. Dorney, could you repeat the question?" Drool leaked down his chin.

"Forget it Plumps, class is over. It's just me." Plumpy uncurled his long frame, stood up out of his desk, stretched his arms, and yawned. With his wild growth of curly blond hair, and his tall skinny frame, he looked more like a sunflower than a Plumpy. Once upon a time, he'd been a heavy kid—and I *do* mean heavy—but when he came back to third grade from his summer vacation a few years before, he'd all of a sudden been skinny as a pole. At the time, we asked him where old Plumpy went, and the name stuck for good. Besides, who wants a best friend named Leonard?

Plumpy and I left the classroom and headed toward our last class of the day: Quilting. As usual, a group of girls had taken over the mirrors in front of one of the hallway make-up stations, and as we passed them, we instinctively held our breath. The week before, I'd seen a new kid walking down the hall. He didn't know about needing to hold your breath. The blast of apple cinnamon perfume that hit him was so potent, it was like he'd walked into an invisible wall. He passed out instantly. Trust me. That's a mistake you only make once.

"That was kind of embarrassing back in class today, didn't you think?" I wanted to gauge Plump's reaction.

Plumpy shrugged. "I slept the whole class, dreamt about a gang of mitochondria taking over a rival cell. So what happened?" he asked.

I wondered if Plumpy might give me an honest opinion. "Hey," I whispered, "do you think that I'm... well... do you think I'm squishy?" I was ready for the worst.

Plumps raised his eyebrows and looked at me like maybe I wasn't feeling well. He scratched his chin with his thumb and forefinger. "Hmmm... not sure about the proper definition of squishy."

I looked around to see if anybody was watching, then, remembering how Dorney had been staring at my middle half, grabbed some of my belly with both hands. "You know... *this*... squishy. Do you think I could stand to lose a few pounds?"

Plumpy was still confused, so I explained what had happened in class while he'd been asleep, dreaming of whatevers taking over a rival thingy. When I finished, he ran both of his hands through his mop of curly blond hair, looked at my belly, and shrugged.

"I guess so."

"You mean it? Seriously? You really think I'm fat?"

"Calm down, Peter. When I was eight, I was fat. You're not fat." He paused, a smile spreading across his face. "You just got a little jiggle in your middle. A little jelly in the belly. A little gummy in the tummy."

"You're having fun, aren't you?"

Plumpy looked hurt. "You *do* realize I'm the kid that everyone calls Plumpy? Besides, who cares what Dorney thinks?"

"I do. She's making me get a diet book from the library and do this big project on losing weight."

"That's ridiculous. Why would she make you do that?"

"Because Jessica gave her the idea."

Plumpy tensed, and his jaw moved like he was grinding his teeth, then he nodded knowingly. He always got that way when the subject of Jessica came up. "First synchro, now this?" He stopped in front of our classroom. "At least we have quilting to take our minds off of it."

"Nah. I'm going to hide from the world in the library and get this over with."

"Suit yourself."

I left Plumpy at class and made my way to the library, where I showed the librarian, Dr. Branless, my pass. Branless was pencil-thin, her skin white as paper, and her straight hair a dull brown. She looked like a cross between a Q-tip and a straw mop. *Not* a welcoming sight.

She read over my pass, then looked at me like I was trying to get away with something. Finally, she initialed the bottom, and, before I could even think of saying anything, she put her finger to her lips.

"Shhhh!"

On the way to the stacks, I passed a couple of girls who were laying flower petals at the foot of the large bronze Helga McMasters statue in the center of the library. McMasters had been the leader of the Correction from like a million years ago, and girls were always leaving flowers for her, sticking little notes in between her feet, rubbing the statue for good luck. None of it made any sense to me. But I was only a boy.

I found the health section, then scanned the shelves until I found a row labeled *Diet Books*. I was studying the titles and squinting when a creaking noise caught my attention and I whirled around.

Nothing. No one. Satisfied I was alone, I browsed the books again, hoping to find something that was just for boys. I found one— literally, *one*. One diet book for boys in the entire library. A strange-looking book titled *A Tale of Two Pounds: A Boy's Guide To A Slimmer Waist.*

Perfect. Not only did I have to do some made-up project in front of everyone, but I had to do it with the most humiliating book in history. Oh, man. Jessica would go crazy when she learned about this. Taking a deep breath, I sat down at a reading table and opened to the first page.

It was the best of fat, it was the worst of fat.

Un—be—lievable. There was no way I could read this. I sat the book down, looked again at what Plumpy called the jiggle in my middle, and took a deep breath, a breath caught somewhere between the floors of sorrow and despair.

I sat there, my hands propped up against my face, staring across the library at the McMasters statue, and wondered why my life had to stink so bad. And then suddenly a thought occurred to me. Why didn't old Helga invite the *boys* of the world to lay flower petals at her feet? I'd never seen a single boy there.

Why was it always about girls?

I returned to the book and noticed something I hadn't seen the first time. Near the top of the first page, handwritten in small blue ink, were three words:

FOLLOW THE CIRCLES

My chest tightened and my throat went dry. I knew this handwriting; had just *seen* this handwriting. I unzipped my backpack, fished out the note, then set it side by side with the book and compared the handwriting.

The same. Exactly the same. The hairs on the back of my neck stood up, and a chill ran down my spine. I stood and spun around, scanning the library, totally freaked out. How was this possible? Somebody puts a note in my locker, a totally weird note, and then this same person has written a note in the same book that I check out?

Get a grip, Peter. I went back to the book, my heart still beating quickly.

FOLLOW THE CIRCLES

If the handwriting was different, I might have thought it was Jessica messing with me, but Jessica couldn't write this badly if her life depended on it. Plus, sneakiness wasn't her style. She was much more likely to hit you in the face with a book than hide weird messages in one. Nope, this secret messenger was playing a dangerous game. Everybody knew writing in books was a serious offense. And what's more, this was blue ink—not even an approved color for boys. But I was definitely intrigued. The question was: What circles was I supposed to follow?

I looked around the library for some clue, and I found one in front of me, hanging high on the wall. A large, circular clock. Could that be it? I walked to the clock and looked up. Short brass hour hand, long brass minute hand, black numbers, glass face. Nothing special about it at all. But the message did say follow the "circles" as in plural. To the right of the clock was a large rectangular air conditioning duct. But to the left, another ten feet down the wall, was a small window. A circular window. And beyond that, another circular window. That had to be it.

I walked along the edge of the wall, my eyes following those windows, when I turned a corner and ran into the last person I wanted to see.

"Well, if it isn't Squishy."

I jumped, the book flying out of my hands and landing in a potted plant a few feet away. I caught my breath and focused on the girl in front of me.

Jessica "the Ice Princess" Hale.

"Jeesh, Peter. Little jumpy today?" She winked. "Let me get that for you." Before I could think, she had the book in her hand and was studying the cover.

She burst out laughing, then covered her mouth. Now she was nodding her head. "This... this is even better than I imagined." Then the laughter gurgled out again. "I cannot *wait* to tell the girls. Priceless, just priceless. Serves you right for not reading *Ophelia* in the first place."

Normally, this is the spot where I would try to insult Jessica in every possible way. But not today. I needed that book back. So I held out my hand.

"What?" she said with a pouty face. "Peter has nothing clever to say?"

"It's bad enough that I have to do this stupid report, okay? Just give me the book and let me get it over with."

"Not so fast," she said as she licked her finger and opened up the book to what I could see was the first page. I stepped toward her, but using the palm of her other hand she punched me in the chest, stopping me in my tracks.

She cleared her throat. "It was the best of fat, it was the worst of fat." Her eyes grew as big as that circular clock, then she burst out laughing again. "This is too good. I almost feel sorry for you, Peter. Almost." She lowered her eyes back to the page. If she saw the blue handwriting, I was a dead man. I had to do something fast. Her eyes were tracking back and forth across the page and she was chuckling to herself.

At the very least, I would get blamed for writing in the book. That was bad enough. But if that note meant something, and she figured it out? I couldn't let that happen.

And so I had to do something that I would almost certainly regret.

I bent low, counted to three in my head, and exploded, running into Jessica as hard as I possibly could. She screamed as she toppled backward, the book flying through the air. But before she could gather herself, my hands were on that book and I was running fast, past a stunned Dr. Branless and away from a screaming Jessica Hale.

I sprinted down the hallway like my life depended on it, because I was certain if Jessica got her hands on me, my life would be over. I raced into the boys' bathroom and locked myself into the last stall. I didn't have much time.

The book said to follow the circles. But did it say anything else? I scanned down the page, sweat dripping off my forehead and landing on the bottom. Right next to a small blue circle.

I wasn't supposed to follow circles on a wall after all. I was supposed to follow circles in the book. The blue circle surrounded the word "the," and when I turned the page, sure enough, there were more blue circles. Circles around the words "world" and "you." On every page, words were circled, and then letters were circled, and then eventually the blue circles stopped. It was like some kind of code. I grabbed a pen out of my pocket and started to write the circled words out on my hand. I heard yelling out in the hallway. Frantic girl yelling. They were close.

As fast as I could, I wrote down every circled world and every circled letter. When I finished, I looked at what I had. And even though the ink was smearing, the message was unmistakable:

The world you know is broken.

The brave are needed to fix it.

The bathroom door flew open, its knob smashing against the concrete block wall. Jessica screamed, "Peter Mills!"

I read the next three words.

Are you brave?

"There, I see some feet." It was Dr. Branless. I read the next three words.

Or are you?

"Peter Mills, are you in the bathroom?"

Uh-oh—that was Principal Lemming's voice. I looked at my hand. Or are you what? No more words. Only letters left.

"I said, Mr. Mills, are you in the bathroom?"

The letters were S, Q, and U—

High heels clicked against the bathroom tile as the women headed right for me.

Then a letter I, followed by an S.

A pounding on the door, one foot from my face.

"Peter Mills, we know you're in there. Now come out immediately."

An H. And a Y.

Someone was shaking the stall door back and forth now.

"Open this door at once, young man!" Principal Lemming screamed.

That was it. No more letters, no more words. I looked at what I had. And suddenly, everything made sense.

THE WORLD YOU KNOW IS BROKEN. THE BRAVE ARE NEEDED TO FIX IT. ARE YOU BRAVE?

Then I swallowed hard, stopped breathing, and felt the tinglies run down my spine.

OR ARE YOU SQUISHY?

The bathroom door was almost shaking off its hinges, the screaming on the other side unbearable. I had no time left. I grabbed a chunk of pages from the book, ripped them off, then balled them up and threw them in the toilet. I flushed just as the door flew open.

Principal Lemming was in the middle, Branless on her left, and Jessica on her right. All three had sweat pouring down their faces. Their hair was messed up, their faces red with anger. And I had only one thing to say.

CHAPTER FOUR

A BUSY BATHROOM

"Can't a guy go the bathroom by himself?"

Principal Lemming had to hold Jessica and Dr. Branless back as both tried to punch me. And I have to say, Principal Lemming was much stronger than she looked. After finally settling both of them down, she said, "Peter, Miss Hale claims you attacked her in the library, and Dr. Branless saw you sprint out of her library trying to steal a book." She pointed. "That book in particular, I presume. What do you have to say for yourself?"

"Guilty as charged."

"I told you," Jessica said triumphantly.

"That's all you have to say for yourself?"

"No, ma'am." I pointed at Jessica. "She's also guilty of something."

Jessica stomped her foot while Lemming raised an eyebrow.

"Really, Mr. Mills. Please tell me, what is Miss Hale guilty of?"

I shrugged. "Being stupendously beautiful."

"Excuse me?"

"Well, look at her, she's practically perfect, like a walking statue of a goddess."

All three women were confused, none more than Jessica.

"And why are you telling us this?"

I held the book up, the cover inches from her face. "Because, Principal Lemming, this is a diet book. I was reading this and dropped it in front of Jessica. And then she started to read it."

"And you apparently lost your mind."

"I admit it, yes. I freaked out, lost my mind. But I did so for a very simple reason: I was embarrassed." I pointed at Jessica again. "Jessica, Jessica Hale, *the* Jessica Hale, the beautiful, stunning vision, prettier-than-a-portrait Jessica Hale, she was reading my diet book."

"I still don't completely follow…"

I pointed to my belly. My shirt stuck out; it looked like I had grown several inches of fat in the last hour. "*This*, Principal Lemming. I'm squishy. I've got a jelly belly, too much jiggle in my middle. *This*. I was embarrassed. I didn't want to steal the book, I didn't want to run over Jessica, but I did… because I was monumentally embarrassed. And because I'm a boy, and sometimes boys can't help themselves."

Principal Lemming scratched her chin. "I can't say I understand, but I see what you're saying, and it makes sense. So you're embarrassed, I get it. Just—give the book back to Dr. Branless and apologize to Jessica and we'll try to forget this ever happened."

I couldn't believe she fell for it.

By the look on her face, neither could Jessica. "Principal Lemming, you can't trust a word Peter says." Principal Lemming cut her off with a wave of her hand. "Enough, Miss Hale. I've already spent more time in a boys' bathroom then I ever wanted to in my life. He's right. You're stunningly beautiful, and he's a boy who needs to lose a few pounds and was embarrassed." She looked back down at my gut. "Maybe more than a few pounds. So let's leave it at that."

"But—"

"Now, Miss Hale, please—before the smell of urine causes me to pass out."

I smiled the least guilty smile I could muster, and Jessica narrowed her eyes at me. The message was clear: the two of us weren't done, not even close. I held my breath as they walked back toward the bathroom door when I heard a gasp. I poked my head out of the stall.

Dr. Branless had stopped, was staring down at the open diet book, and was shaking.

Uh-oh.

She turned and pointed at me. "He—he—he ruined this book." Principal Lemming was looking now. "Look! He tore pages from my book!"

Principal Lemming grabbed the book and raced right toward me. She shook the book in my face.

"And am I to believe that Miss Hale's beauty is also the reason you tore a hunk of pages out of this book?"

I shook my head and swallowed hard. "That, actually, is even more embarrassing. You see, I was in the stall, trying to use the bathroom, when all of you barged in and demanded I get out. Well, before I could open the door, I had to, er, finish... and well... as you can see..." I pointed at the toilet paper dispenser.

The *empty* toilet paper dispenser.

"There really was no way for me to finish without..." I pointed at the book.

Principal Lemming was confused. Then slowly the confusion changed to recognition. And then all of a sudden she was disgusted. "For the love of Helga McMasters', now I really *am* going to pass out." She shook her head. "Dr. Branless, just have Mr. Drummond fix the book and let's leave this ridiculous boy alone before I hear anything else that might make me get sick."

I held my breath as they left the bathroom. When I was absolutely certain they weren't coming back, I collapsed on the toilet seat and couldn't help but smile. I lifted up my shirt and pulled out the full roll of toilet paper I'd stuffed in there.

Like I said before: When in trouble, best to play the loser card.

After school, I wandered outside and saw the usual dozen or so bright pink buses lined up at the curb. Fabulous, I thought to myself. I heard the happy (and annoying!) giggling of the hundreds of girls swarming the school commons. Then I watched an equal number of boys dotting the grounds. Yet, to everyone but me, the boys were invisible: walking in silence, hands in pockets, shoulders slumped, carrying overloaded backpacks. They trudged toward those pink buses like they were actually pink tombs. In a way, I guess they were.

I trudged along myself toward the number fifteen bus, which took me home each day. All I could think about was the message I'd found.

The world you know is broken. The brave are needed to fix it.

Are you brave? Or are you squishy?

None of it made any sense. I had been called "squishy" less than thirty minutes before I'd found the diet book in the library. Which meant someone had worked ridiculously fast to get me a message. But who?

"Hey, freak! Snap out of it!"

I looked up and saw the horrifying face of Margie, our bus driver. She was chewing down on something hard; I couldn't tell if it was gum, her own tongue, or some asphalt from the parking lot. The dark stubble growing on her upper lip was matched in creepiness only by the single long dark hair growing out of the big brown mole on her cheek. (Plumpy and I had a betting pool revolving around how long that hair would grow.) Her purple eye shadow was thick and bright, and I sometimes wondered whether she bought it at a makeup counter or a hardware store. Somehow, the school district had found the scariest person in the world to drive my bus. And today, something was wrong. She had a weird grin on her face—not a good sign. And then she spoke.

"Hurry it up, Squishy."

The bus exploded in girl laughter. Margie slapped her knee like she'd just said the funniest thing in the world, then she even high-fived one of Jessica's friends who was standing right behind her. Probably the defining moment in Margie's life.

The first couple minutes of the bus drive home were filled with a constant chorus of "Squishy, Squishy," chanted in an annoying, sing-songy sort of way. The final ten minutes of the trip were filled up with a rousing rendition of the new instant classic, "Ninety-Nine Bottles of Fat On The Wall."

That night at dinner, I poked at some lumpy green and white stuff, lost in thought. Out of nowhere, the front door opened, there was a click-clack of heels, and suddenly there was that "six-o'clock feeling" in the house. You know, when *she* came home.

"Harold!" my mother yelled, never breaking stride. "Peter better be—"

She walked into the kitchen and spotted me sitting at the table, right where I was every evening when she came home from work.

"Good," she said, shaking her head at me. Then she sniffed the air, apparently catching a whiff of the green and white stuff, and shook her head again. She grabbed the mail from the kitchen counter and sat down, ripping open mail furiously and reading through it at the speed of light, while Dad and I continued to sit in silence.

Finally, she shuffled the mail back into a neat pile and turned her attention to me. My heart stopped.

"So, imagine my surprise. I'm in the middle of approving copy for a new email campaign when I get a phone call from your school." My mother's eyes were burning holes in my face.

I could have made this relatively painless on myself. I could have told her I was sorry, I was an idiot, I was an embarrassment upon her and all the other peoples of the world. I could have, but I didn't. I was, as they say, on a roll.

"Let me guess. Did Principal Lemming call you to tell you I made the Honors Society again?"

My mother narrowed her eyes at me.

"What is that? Is that your attempt at humor? Where exactly did you learn that? From those boys you run around with at school? I give you everything you could possibly want"—she gestured in the direction of what I could only assume was everything I could possibly want—"and this is the thanks I get? A boy who mocks authority, that's what I get. Aren't I right, Harold?" She invoked my father's name, but she was still staring at me.

My dad, like usual, looked frozen in a pose I liked to call hopelessly awkward. He grunted something that sounded like water bubbling out of the garbage disposal, or maybe a coffee maker beginning to perk.

"It appears that our Peter was *once again* unprepared for his Great Books class. Mrs. Dorney said, and I quote, 'Peter tried to fake preparedness for oral questions today.' *Fake preparedness?* I'm not sure I've ever even heard of something like that. Do you have any idea how poorly that reflects on me as a mother? As a woman? Fake preparedness, my purse. Tonight you can scrub the kitchen floor with a toothbrush while you think about 'faking preparedness' next time."

At least she hadn't gotten a call about the library incident. If she had, I'd be scrubbing the outside of the house as well. Like I said, I could have made that easier on myself. But when you're on a roll, you're on a roll.

I spent the rest of the night on my hands and knees. Toothbrush scrubbing was my mother's default punishment, and I'd gotten rather good at it through the years. I was almost done when I heard mother yell at my dad.

"Harold, go get the antifungal cream! My toes have been burning like mad today!"

I heard feet on the steps and then my dad popped into the kitchen, wearing his plaid pajamas. He shrugged his shoulders at me (for all boys and fathers have their own secret code as well), then grabbed the medicine tin from under our cabinet and started looking for Mom's special cream.

I wondered if I would be like my dad someday. I had wondered it before. No doubt I would probably wonder it again. Would I be married to a woman who didn't appear to like me? Would I spend my days cooking slimy food with no taste? Would the best part of my day be creating a new quilted pillow that I could show off down at Bernie's store?

I guess all those wonderings is what led me to ask.

"Dad." He stopped and turned to me.

"Yes, Peter."

"Do you think the world is broken?"

His eyes grew big and he looked around.

"What would make you ask something like that?"

I shrugged. "Don't know. It's just, you know, things seem out of whack sometimes. Don't you think?"

Dad looked at me with his kind and gentle brown eyes. He took a few little breaths. It looked like he was trying to think of what to say… or, if I was lucky, how to say it.

"HAROLD! They're on fire, literally on fire! Get up here with my cream now!"

Dad took a deep breath, shook his head like he had a shiver, and walked back upstairs without saying a word.

As I lay awake in my bed that night, I replayed the day's events in my head. I laughed about Lemming's face when she finally figured out what I'd used those pages from the book for. She rebounded well, though, telling Dr. Branless that Mr. Drummond, the bookbinder, would fix that book.

Then it hit me.

Something I hadn't put together until just now. When I'd first gotten to the health section and started looking for a diet book, I heard something. I definitely heard something.

A creaking.

CHAPTER FIVE

THE DUNGEON

On any normal day, I (and the one hundred percent of my body that disliked pain) would have stumbled around school, dreading the first synchronized swimming practice and whatever torture The Falcon had in store for us.

But this was not a normal day.

Because I knew where that creaking came from.

The basement under the library was more affectionately known as "the dungeon." It was the place where the school's bookbinder worked. Mr. Drummond—or "Bad Breath Drummond," as we called him. One time I foolishly bumped into him in the hall, and his breath had been so bad, I still had nightmares about it. Drummond's job was to make certain every book in the building had a good, strong leather binding. Although he spent most of his time in his dungeon working, once a day, Drummond came upstairs and pushed his old cart around school, looking for damaged books.

And if you were a student at Finley Junior High, you always knew when Drummond was coming close, because his old book cart creaked.

Drummond must have been in the health section right before I got there. He could have written the message in that book. And he was a boy, so the handwriting fit. I had no idea how he could have found out about my new nickname so fast, but at this point, I had no other clue to go on.

And so it was back to the library.

When I arrived, Dr. Branless was up on a stool, shelving books. She looked down at me and hissed, a horrified expression crossing her face.

"You?"

"Dr. Branless, I came to apologize."

"Just get out, okay?"

"And Principal Lemming thought it might be a good idea if I go down to the dungeon and help Mr. Drummond fix the book I screwed up."

She squinted at me, then started nodding her head. "You, all alone in the dungeon with Mr. Drummond? Yes, that is a fitting punishment." She pointed to the far side of the library. "Try not to destroy anything on your way."

On the far side of the library I found an old elevator with one yellow button. I pushed it, a faint bell sounded, and the doors opened slowly and unevenly. I walked in and pushed the down button. The one labeled "Bookbinding."

The elevator lurched back and forth, groaned and squeaked, but then it straightened out, hit bottom, and the doors opened up into the dark basement: the dungeon. A few lamps were lit, but the room still felt dark and shadowy. The cool air smelled like old wet shoes. As the elevator doors shut behind me, I wondered if this was such a good idea.

"State your business, whoever you are."

Too late.

It was Drummond all right, and his voice was raspy and hoarse. Either he'd damaged his vocal cords years ago, or he was trying to sound like the kind of guy who liked spending all his time in a creepy dark dungeon.

"Hello? Mr. Drummond?"

"Come around."

I made my way around tall stacks of books and found Drummond hunched over an enormous book, gluing the binding back together. He held his hand up for me to stop.

"This is the most important moment of all. If the glue bonds and we get proper binding fusion, then we don't have to start with new leather. You always want to preserve the original binding if you can—it's the first rule of bookbinding."

I leaned in closer to see what he was doing. "I thought the first rule of bookbinding is that you do not talk about bookbinding."

I don't think he heard me.

"Wait for it… wait for it… wait for it… hot slappity dog!" He slammed his fist to the table in triumph. He turned around and took off the magnifying lens he was wearing around his forehead, then took his regular glasses from around his neck, put them on, leaned forward, and stared at me. "Ah, Peter Mills."

As soon as his mouth opened, his breath hit me like a sledgehammer—a sledgehammer wrapped in an old sweaty sock filled with cat poop. Like his breath had actually ripened into an even more terrible vintage of nasty since the day I'd bumped into him in the hall.

He grunted at me.

I looked around to make sure nobody was around. Then my lower lip started to hurt, and I realized it was because I was chewing on it nervously.

Drummond laughed. "You've got nothing to worry about down here. There's a reason I keep it kind of creepy." He squinted his eyes, stared up to the ceiling, and pointed with his index finger. "Keeps them away."

He motioned for me to sit down.

"So, you know me?" I asked.

"Yep, I know you."

He folded his arms and studied me. So I studied him back. Drummond had lots of hair, but unfortunately for him, most of it was coming out of his ears. The little hair that still grew out of his head sprouted up in little grey patches, making Drummond look like a strange spotted creature. One of his eyebrows seemed to arch up higher than the other, his eyes were dull brown, and you couldn't look at his teeth without getting woozy. Drummond was the sort of guy who made ugly men feel better about themselves.

"We can have a staring contest, if you like. Or you can start talking," Drummond said.

"Did you send me a message?" I asked.

"I did."

I steadied myself. "Why? What does it all mean?"

"I think you know what it means. I think you've always known."

"But you… you're wrong, I don't have any idea."

Drummond laughed. "Really? You have *no* idea. Truth is, I think you're just *afraid* of what it all means."

This stupid message had caused me a lot of grief. I wanted to know what he was doing. "Why did you send this message to *me*?"

"Why you?" He laughed again, opened up a desk drawer and pulled out a file. He licked his thumbs—a shot of nastiness escaping from his mouth—and opened up the file.

"Here's why. You came to my attention three years ago. I heard some scuttlebutt in the faculty lounge about how you'd been sassing back to young Jessica Hale. Apparently it was bad enough that Mrs. Hale called the school to complain. You annoy an important woman like Margo Hale? That gets my attention. I came by your classroom not long after that to test you. I did a presentation on how to fix the binding on a set of books. An old set of *Tilda Toobers*."

"I remember. You asked for volunteers."

Drummond nodded. "You came up, helped me fuse a binding, and I knew it right then. I knew you had the gift."

"For bookbinding?"

"Among other things. But still, you weren't yet ready, so I sat back and observed. And—oh my—have you built up quite a file. Multiple calls home to your mother every year, for all manner of infractions, and a consistent ability to confront and battle Finley's most powerful and influential student, Jessica Hale. Peter, that's the portrait of a boy who's dissatisfied with life but who—instead of climbing into a hole, and this is where you're exceptional—is willing to fight back."

"You've been *watching* me?" I didn't know whether to be impressed or creeped out. "How is that even possible? How could you know what was said during our classes, during phone calls?"

He smirked and pointed straight up at the ceiling. "Peter, they have no idea what I do down here. They think, 'Weird old guy plays with his books and his glue.' He spun at his desk and pulled open a couple of drawers. They revealed a bank of radios with different plugs. He pushed a button and turned up the volume.

It was the familiar chatter from the cafeteria.

"I've got the whole school wired for sound," he said. "I can listen in on any classroom, any office, and most phone calls. I've been listening to you, too. And I think you've got what it takes."

"To do what?"

"Finally know the truth."

I stood up, trying to process what was going on. "But why now? If you've been watching and listening to me all this time, then why now?"

"It's not every day a kid gets called 'Squishy' by his teacher. Oh, and I heard The Falcon just put you on the synchronized swimming team. Ha, that's funny stuff. Peter, in my experience, sometimes people fight hardest when they're at their lowest."

I closed my eyes and took a long slow breath, then opened them up again. "What do you want from me?"

"I want you to make a choice. Either learn the real truth, or go on with your life and stop complaining. That's what I want. I want you to make a choice."

"I don't understand."

Drummond took an envelope out of the folder, then pulled a key off his keychain.

He held the key up.

"If you want to know the real truth about our world, you choose the key. It opens a door. Step inside the door and have your questions answered. On the other hand… if you're scared and you'd rather just go on living your life, like your dad and so many like him," Drummond shrugged, "then you choose the envelope."

"What's in the envelope?"

Drummond shook his head. "That's not how this works. You have to choose for yourself."

"And the key?"

"Like I said. The real truth."

"How long do I have to make the choice?"

"How about ten seconds? And this is a one-time offer."

I held the envelope in my hand and tapped my toe against the dungeon floor.

"I really don't want to end up like my dad."

"Five seconds."

I handed the envelope back to Drummond and grabbed the key out of his hand.

"Show me this door."

CHAPTER SIX

THE REAL TRUTH

I followed Drummond as he weaved through a maze of old books. Most stacks were six to eight feet tall, old brown leather edges hanging out, signs of bindings that had seen better days. And the stacks themselves looked to be spread out with no real order, probably to maximize the "shabby chic" look that creeps in basements often go for.

And the smell, although an improvement over Drummond's breath, wasn't what you'd call a sign of *fresh* air. More like the stench of wet clothes when they sit in the back of a car too long.

Bad Breath Drummond led me to a corner, where I could make out an old lamp and an empty crate. He flipped the lamp on, its half-burnt bulb barely lighting up the corner space, then took his binding knife out of his pocket, showed it to me, and ran it along his tongue. Very comforting.

He wedged the knife between two bricks in the wall and worked loose one of the bricks. Then he reached his hand into the hole left by the brick and appeared to grab something. He pulled hard and started to walk backward. Incredibly, part of the wall swung with him. Like a door.

"A door made out of bricks?"

"The door itself is steel. I just bricked it over to hide it."

"But if all you did was pull, then why do I need this key?"

I was apparently too busy being awed by the brick-steel door to notice that the first door merely revealed another door. This one was solid steel. And it had a keyhole.

I placed the key in the hole until something clicked. Then I turned it. There was a squeaking, then finally another click, and the door pushed forward, releasing a draft of cool air.

Drummond nodded his head slightly, and together we walked through to the other side. He hit a switch, and small electric lights lit up a cramped little cave that had been dug out and braced with wooden timbers and cement.

"Did *you* do all this?

He nodded.

"It's incredible," I said, imagining how long it had taken him to build all this, and wondering exactly why he had bothered.

He led me across the cave and through a tunnel. It extended maybe fifteen feet and then ballooned into a slightly larger room, almost circular, maybe ten feet across. The walls were lined with photographs, and a variety of objects lay around the edges of the room, leaning up against the rounded walls.

"What is all this?"

"This, Peter, is the real truth."

I spun around the room, scanning the pictures for something familiar. My eye was drawn to the largest photograph in the room. I knew the woman featured in it. It was the most famous woman in the world.

Helga McMasters.

Throughout my life, I'd seen hundreds of photographs, paintings, and statues of McMasters. But never this one. She was dressed in an all-white uniform. Behind her were hundreds of other women, also dressed in white, standing board-stiff in perfectly aligned rows.

I turned to Drummond.

"What is this picture?"

"You've got to understand: we don't know many details. They've done a remarkable job of keeping us in the dark."

"About what?"

"The truth."

This was getting frustrating.

"All we've got is fragments, Peter. Take this, for instance." He reached down and grabbed a hard green hat. He put it on my head and blasted the top of my head with his fist.

"Ouch. What the?"

"It's called a helmet. And from the inscription inside, it looks like it comes from a place called France."

"I don't understand. What does that mean?"

Drummond ignored my question, walked a few more feet, and grabbed something else. A framed photo. It showed a tall, dark-haired man wearing a blue suit and red tie; he was standing in front of an enormous room making a speech. Two men stood behind him, and most of the people in the audience were men.

"Strange, ain't it?" said Drummond. He was already bent down, grabbing something else.

"Strange is an understatement. Is this some kind of old-time quilting bee?" I asked, trying to make some sense of the picture.

"And how about this?" Drummond said while handing me another frame, this one much larger. This frame didn't hold a picture. Rather, under the glass were several scraps of old brown paper, each partially torn. On the scraps was writing, in cursive, but not the overly loopy form I was used to from girls. This cursive was boy writing. Yet somehow not messy.

My eyes were drawn to the scrap in the middle of the frame.

That among these are life, liberty, and the pursuit of happiness

Drummond was watching me. "Weird?"

"Definitely," I said.

"And that's not even the strangest part. Look here." He pointed down to the bottom.

The cursive was harder to read here. It looked like people's signatures, but they were tough to make out.

And then, as I examined them, something became clear. Something very strange. They appeared to be the signatures of men. *Only* men.

The largest one, above the others, was much easier to read.

"John Hancock? Mr. Drummond, who the heck was this?" I said, tapping on the glass frame.

All he could do was shrug.

"Then what does it mean?"

He shrugged again.

"I don't understand. You said I would find the truth down here. All you've done is shown me a bunch of things I've never seen before in my life, things that don't make any sense to me."

Drummond's face lit up, like I'd just gotten the answer to a difficult question.

"Isn't it strange that you've never seen these things before?"

He bent down again and picked up another picture, blew dust off the glass frame. "This is the oldest picture I've got."

This one was the strangest yet, and it was impossible to make sense of it. Thousands of… of men, all dressed in the same identical uniform. Sort of like that McMasters photo. Each man was holding something long and brown at his side. Each one stood ramrod straight. In front of them, five other men rode atop horses. Long metal swords hung from their sides.

The picture made me nervous. "This isn't a quilting bee, is it?"

Drummond shook his head. "I know a guy in the brotherhood, claims it was an army. Can you imagine? A man's army. Said those men were all holding rifles, guns. And as you can tell from the picture, that's one seriously big army."

I looked at it again and noticed some writing at the very bottom of the picture. I blew the remaining dust off and looked more closely. I almost lost my breath.

Ottoman Turkish Empire

Turkish? Izmir would go absolutely nuts if he saw this.

"There's something else I'd like you to see." Drummond motioned for me to join him at a small square table. On top of the table was a grey bundle, which Drummond unwrapped, revealing a large book. The leather cover and binding seemed unusually thick, and on the front cover, three letters were engraved:

B – A – M

"Bam?"

"No, Peter, it's an acronym. Any ideas what the letters might stand for?"

I studied it carefully; placed my finger against the letters and traced them. B. A. M. The only thing that came to mind was a theme for a birthday party I had when I turned ten.

"Buttons and Mints?" I said.

Drummond slammed his fist against the wall. Bits of dust came down from overhead. "Oh, for flip's sake, Peter! Be A Man. Peter, it stands for *BE A MAN.*"

Wow, that was way better than buttons and mints.

"Peter, us bookbinders go through all the books. That's our job. And you know what we sometimes find? Scraps, pieces of paper, notes, and pictures left to us from… long ago."

I started to flip open The Book, but Drummond's hand came down and shut the cover tight.

"Not yet. Peter, I need to know if I can trust you."

"Of course you can trust me."

"I trust the Bookbinding Brotherhood. If you're going to look at this book, then you need to enter the Brotherhood first."

For a moment I wondered if this meant I had to work in the library someday, refuse to bathe, and be scary and repulsive.

Drummond seized my wrists. He pulled me close, and his old-sock sledgehammer breath hit me again. I gagged.

"Peter, are you willing to take the Bookbinder's Oath?"

I held my breath and nodded yes.

He let go of my wrists, grabbed The Book, and turned it toward me so the binding faced up. He grabbed my hand and placed it on the binding.

His eyes went all scary on me, and his breathing grew deep.

"Repeat after me:

Upon this old book's glorious edge

I do solemnly here pledge

To make my words be straight and true

Or turn me into binding glue."

I repeated the words, not missing even one. Drummond gave me a goofy look, grabbed me by the shoulders, and shook me.

"Proud of you, Peter. This day's been a long time coming. Time for you to get to work."

"Work?"

"Yes, you have an important role to play."

"Which is?"

"You're gonna help change the world."

I gulped.

"I'm a binder, Peter. I keep a memory of the past. But I'm not a *changer*. I've been looking for a changer, someone to lead that fight. *You're* the changer, Peter."

"But Mr. Drummond, I still don't even know what's going on. You said I would learn the truth, but all you've shown me is a bunch of weird stuff."

Drummond cocked his head to the side, squinted his eyes, and put his finger to his mouth. He jogged through the tunnel and back out into the dungeon. A phone was ringing. He answered it, said "Be right there," and hung up.

"Sorry Peter, I'm needed upstairs. Binding emergency on the newest edition of the *Flemency Foyle Poodle Detective* books. And I'm sorry to say I can't leave you down here alone."

He grabbed The Book out of my hands and bundled it up once more with grey cloth. Then he unzipped my backpack, put it inside, zipped the bag up again, and patted me on the shoulder.

"Looks like you're ready, Peter. Remember: read The Book, learn everything you can, then change things. And check in with me down here. Let me know how everything's going."

"But Mr. Drummond, I don't even know what you're talking about."

He was dragging me to the elevator. "Sure you do, Peter. You've known for quite some time. That's why I chose you."

We took the elevator back up to the library and stepped off. He walked one way and I walked another. Then he spun around.

"Oh, and Peter. I think I forgot to tell you something about the Brotherhood, and now that you have The Book, it's important to mention it."

"Yeah?" I said, more than a little freaked out.

"If someone catches you with The Book, then the entire Brotherhood could unravel. Everything could be ruined."

My chest tightened. "Which means?"

"Better to die than let a woman get her hands on that book."

CHAPTER SEVEN

SYNCHRO

I sat in my next class, backpack stuck between my legs, scared out of my mind and wondering what I'd gotten myself into. Though I didn't always enjoy my life, I rather enjoyed *living*—the breathing in and out part. If Drummond had sent me a cryptic message with the words, "You may need to sacrifice your life for a big leather book," I'm not so sure I would have found my way down to the dungeon.

I did everything I could that afternoon not to bring attention to myself. I tried the "sleeping with my eyes open" trick, the "look for pencils under my desk" trick, and one time I even cried a little when a teacher asked a question. I'd never resorted to crying in class to avoid a question before, but this situation called for drastic measures. I felt like the weight of the entire world lay in my backpack, even though it was only an old book about buttons and mints. Er, I mean, being a man.

I got lucky with my very last class of the day. The teacher showed us a video on how to coordinate our wardrobe with our skin tones. As I already knew from my dad that I was a warm autumn and looked best in dark reds and greens, I was able to ignore the video and spend the period watching the clock tick closer to three.

When the end-of-school bell finally rang, I jumped out of my seat and jogged out the door, down the hallway toward the exit. I was looking left and right, trying to make sure nobody was looking at me odd, when out of nowhere I slammed smack dab into something solid and fell backward onto the floor. Wounded but still alive. I looked up.

The Falcon glared down at me.

"You weren't thinking of skipping your very first synchronized swimming practice, were you?"

I had completely forgotten about synchro practice, and there was no way I could do it now. I needed to get The Book to safety.

"Sorry, Coach, I'm just not feeling very well today." I hit my chest with my fist. "Think I ate some bad Brussels sprouts at lunch. Anyway, I need to go home and lie down, but I'll be sure to be at practice tomorrow, because I can't wait to get started."

The Falcon narrowed her eyes. Then she shot her hand down at me, grabbed my shirt, and yanked me off the ground. She turned me around and pointed me in the direction of the swimming pool.

"Peter, only the most pathetic boy would use bad Brussels sprouts as an excuse to get out of synchro, and you're only marginally pathetic. Practice is *that* way. But don't worry, I can walk with you."

The Falcon set her hand on the back of my neck as if she sensed I might bolt for the nearest exit given the opportunity. "No, Peter, you're just scared. And that's nothing to be ashamed of, because, well, you're a boy. Always remember this, Peter: for the weaker gender, bravery isn't the absence of fear. It's a boy doing something *in spite of* his fear."

Even though I was pretty sure The Falcon had just insulted me, what she said made sense.

"But get this, Peter, boys aren't the only ones who get scared." She looked around real quick. "Even I get scared."

"Really?"

"Sure. Now, I'd rather this not get around, but there was this one time, I was driving my Camaro north of town a few years back, and my baby broke down. So here I was on the side of the road, and I'm under my car trying to fix her. And you know what happened? Something sharp and wet grabbed hold of my ankle and started dragging me out from under the car. I look up, and darned if I'm not being dragged through the trees by a full-grown grizzly bear."

"You're kidding me!"

"I am not. Well, that bear, he finally let go of me, and I stood up—and then he pinned me against a pine tree. I thought I was a goner for sure."

"And is that when you were scared?"

She laughed and shook her head. "No, just wait. Well I figured, before this bear eats me I might as well go down swinging, so first thing I did was headbutt him in the nose, then I poked him in the eyes, and then I kneed him in the groin. Did all three, like *wham, boom, bam!* Bear didn't know what hit him. He started holding his eyes with one paw and swinging those deadly claws with his other paw, the funniest thing you ever saw. So I just ran around him, climbed up his back, jumped on his head, and gave him the old choke hold until he passed out cold."

"How did you choke out a bear?"

The Falcon looked offended. She stopped and lifted her left shirt sleeve, flexed her bicep. Across the muscle was a green tattoo with the word "Harry." Then she lifted her right shirt sleeve and showed me another green tattoo, but with the word "Sally."

"Peter, as soon as I brought my guns to the party, it was 'Say Adios to the Big Angry Bear' Time. Nope, some of my friends remember it as the day I defeated a bear. But to me it's much simpler than that. It's the day when Harry met Sally." And right on cue, The Falcon kissed Harry and then Sally. The double biceps kiss: her patented move.

"But I don't understand—you said you were scared. What part of it scared you?"

"Oh, I almost forgot. So I come out of the forest and walk back to my car, when I see another car pulled up next to the Camaro. Three young men were leaning against my hood pointing at my car like a bunch of fools."

"And?"

"And obviously, Peter, that's when I got scared. I thought those idiots were scratching up my paint job."

We arrived at the foyer to the new swimming complex. On one side was a brand-new trophy case that I knew The Falcon would want to fill. On the other side, Eddie the foreman was putting up a big wooden plaque. The Falcon went over and yelled at Eddie about something, and I noticed Eddie go into a weird mouth-half-open kind of a look. Then she snapped her fingers and Eddie shook his head, turned around, and walked away. The Falcon stood there staring at that plaque and that's when I recognized what was on it: an image of her dog, Vicious.

A single tear formed on The Falcon's cheek as she used her shirt sleeve to polish the plaque and then whispered something to her left bicep. Vicious had died the previous year when a fire burned down the former swim building while he was tied to the bleachers. The Falcon had been busy pounding out laps in the pool at the time, the fire raging around her. When asked by Principal Lemming how it was that she hadn't felt the fire, The Falcon told her she'd thought it was simply the heat coming from her sweet workout.

As I pushed the double doors open, the humidity of the pool hit me. The pool complex wasn't finished yet, but one look around made it clear that the entire building would be awfully impressive when it was done. I walked around the pool—it was ready for use, even though the surrounding complex had a ways to go—and stepped inside the boys' locker room, where I found a locker with my name on it.

I debated what to do—there was simply no good way out of this mess. I had to get through synchro and find a way to protect The Book at the same time. As I thought about it, I heard a familiar whimpering from another row of lockers.

"Gary, is that you?"

"They're just so horrible," Gary answered.

Izmir muttered an angry word in Turkish. Probably cursing. Then I remembered the swimsuits.

I grabbed my locker door, took a deep breath, and looked inside. Oh, my.

The swimsuit was a shiny pink, with silver edging, ruffles that bordered the leg holes, and a little pouf that hung on the back of the suit like a tail. Next to the suit hung a pair of nose plugs, goggles, and a shiny pink swim cap.

I wished I knew how to curse in Turkish.

But I could handle this. If The Falcon fought a bear, then I could wear a silly one-piece. I approached the act of putting on the swimsuit like I'd approach pulling off a Band-Aid—or death by beheading. The quicker the better. I grabbed the suit, laid it on the floor, then stepped into it and pulled it up as fast as I could.

One humiliating moment later, I stumbled backward, hit the locker room bench, flipped completely over, and landed on my back for the second time in the last ten minutes.

Maybe doing this quickly wasn't the right approach. And so I tried again. And again. It total, it took me eight tries before I successfully got all my feet and hands in the correct holes. Wearing a girl's swimsuit was exhausting. And practice hadn't even started yet.

I ran my thumbs under the straps and pulled up, then ran my hands down the one-piece, making sure that whatever squish I had wasn't too noticeable. My very first thought—one that I knew I would never, ever share with another human being—was that the suit felt… well… the suit felt good. It was silky smooth to the skin. I noticed a mirror to my left, and walked over and took a long look. Not too shabby at all. I might just be able to pull this off.

Then I heard a cough, the sort that lets you know you're not alone and so you should make sure you don't do anything embarrassing. I spun around and saw Gary, Izmir, and Plumpy standing there in their own pink swimsuits.

"Peter, you weren't just checking yourself out, were you?" Plumpy asked.

Okay, that was embarrassing.

"How many times did it take you before you got your swimsuit on correctly?" I shot back.

"Fourteen," Plumpy said as his face fell.

"Then shut up and get out to the pool. I'll be there in a minute."

I waited until they left, then grabbed my backpack. No way was I going to let it out of my sight. Rumor was that Mr. Ronson, the janitor, liked to snoop through people's bags during gym class. I wasn't going to give him the opportunity. I would need to find a way to keep an eye on my bag during practice.

I walked out to the pool area, scanned the deck, and noticed a large pile of red kickboards against the enormous glass wall that separated the pool from the outside. After looking around to make sure nobody was watching, I hid the bag under the pile. I would keep an eye on the kickboards during practice.

I joined the other guys over near the pool, and together we watched the girls file out of their locker room. I shook my head; I looked just like them. Except that maybe I was a little squishier. If I hadn't been sitting on the world's greatest secret, this would have officially been the lowest of the low points in my short, miserable life.

The Falcon came out of the locker room last, strutting as usual, her shirt sleeves rolled up to show off her muscles, a clipboard in her hand. She blew a whistle.

"Bring it in, bring it in! Okay, let me get a look at you. Good, Peter and the gang, good to see you boys could join us. Girls, looking good. As you probably know, for the last few years, our synchro team has not done as well as I would like. Certainly not up to Falcon standards."

A loud roaring noise started up and we all turned. Eddie the foreman was drilling into a metal beam. Falcon started yelling at him but he couldn't hear her. Finally, she flung her clipboard at him like a Frisbee, hitting him square in the back of his hardhat. He flinched, turned off the drill, and spun around. The Falcon threw a quick double biceps pose his way and screamed. He got the message and ran outside.

"As I was saying: this year, with the regional meet coming here to Finley, we can't have anything but the best. For Finley, but also for Vicious. After last year's fire, I was able to gather the ashes from what I think was Vicious, and I had them added into the concrete that was used in the new building. That's right. So that adorable pooch can always be with us. Also, you may have noticed we are one girl shy, and that's because she deserves a special introduction."

Which girl could possibly deserve a special introduction?

"I had to beg, borrow, and steal her off the girl's track team, and we'll have to share her with Miss Marmalade's Mixed Martial Arts School…"

Oh no, this couldn't possibly be happening.

CHAPTER EIGHT

PROTECTING THE PACK

The girls' locker room door burst open and Jessica Hale, the Ice Princess of the sixth grade, came through wearing her own pink swimsuit and silver designer sunglasses. Since this was an indoor pool, I wasn't exactly sure why she was wearing sunglasses, but I had to admit, she looked a lot better in her swimsuit than Gary or Izmir did.

"Jessica! Thank you so much for joining our squad this year. We are beyond fortunate to have someone of your caliber."

I couldn't imagine what being a snotty know-it-all had to do with synchronized swimming, but apparently even The Falcon was susceptible to Jessica's charms.

Jessica took off her shades. "Oh, no problem at all, Ms. Falcon. It's my pleasure. After I went to Synchro Nationals when I was nine, I decided to branch out into other sports, but I've always kept an eye on the synchro team here at school. And you're right when you say they haven't been performing at Falcon standards. And *certainly* not up to Jessica Hale standards."

I couldn't believe Jessica was good at synchro too. It just wasn't possible.

"I like your gumption, Miss Hale. And I hope it's not asking too much, but I'm going to count on you to step up and lead the team this year, show them what you know, what it takes to be a winner."

Jessica looked right at me.

"Don't worry, Ms. Falcon, it will be my pleasure to lead the members of this squad. I know several of them need a lot of help." She said it like she was chewing me up.

Falcon blew her whistle, told us all to jump in the water, then handed her whistle to Jessica.

"Coach 'em up, Captain Hale."

Jessica put the whistle around her neck and began shouting instructions. "Today is all about sculls and eggbeaters! We're gonna work on them till you puke!"

Jessica explained how sculls are little hand movements used to move the body around. And eggbeaters? Sort of the way a synchro swimmer keeps from drowning. It's a way to tread water using only your feet, which I figured out quickly is just about impossible. Arms, it turns out, are rather helpful for swimming.

I did the best I could for the next ten minutes, but honestly all I could concentrate on was keeping my eyes on the big pile of kickboards, making sure The Book was still safe.

As we practiced, Jessica swam around from person to person, so she could—in her words—"help each of us reach our potential." And if by "reach our potential" she meant insult our brains out, then she was doing an excellent job.

I first saw her go up to Izmir. "Izmir! A weird name for a weird-looking guy doing the oddest sculls I've ever seen. Are you sure those are sculls, or are you making hand puppets in the water?" Even from across the pool, I could see Izmir chewing through the side of his mouth.

Next she went over to Plumpy. "You call that an eggbeater? How do you even stay above water with such an awful eggbeater? Maybe there's more to your name than I realized." I saw her blow her cheeks up real big, and I don't think I've ever seen Plumpy get angry that fast.

Then she found Gary. Well, sort of. "What's your name, kid? And who let you into our pool?"

"It's Gary," he mumbled, gulping up a mouthful of water.

She apparently didn't hear him. "Well, Larry, I've never seen you before, and I'm not sure I want to with sculls like that. And your eggbeaters make me want to cry. I expect better next time, Mary."

"It's Gary," he said again. His head went under the water.

Now she was heading my way. She paused to yell something at Plumpy, and as she did I spotted something out of the corner of my eye: Ronson, the janitor. He'd just come out of the boys' locker room and was now snooping around the pool deck, wandering about as if he was trying to find something to do. For a moment Ronson looked like he was about to move on, and then he spotted the big pile of kickboards over by the wall.

He shook his head.

Uh-oh. He was going over there to clean them up! I had to act quickly.

"Hey! Eyes over here, Squishy."

Jessica. I spun around.

"So, what part of eggbeater didn't you understand? Move it!" she yelled at me.

I didn't have time for a plan, but a really stupid idea flashed in my mind, so I went with it. Screaming like a maniac, I started to swallow as much water as possible. I splashed around like a crazy person, screaming "help!" Then I blew all my air out and sank like a rock to the bottom of the pool.

Yep, fake drowning was my best idea. I sure hoped the distraction would work. Hopefully Ronson wouldn't be able to clean the deck while a kid was dying at the bottom of the pool.

But I didn't have any time to wonder. Next thing I knew, I looked up and saw Jessica darting through the water like a dolphin. She reached me before I could even think about what to do next. She threw her arm around my neck, jerked me upward, and pulled me straight up to the surface.

When we broke through the water, I tried to get some air, but it was hard to breathe with Jessica crushing my windpipe with her forearm. I looked around for Ronson, and sure enough he'd left the kickboards behind; he was now at the side of the pool, tossing a life preserver in our direction. I sneaked a peek at the messy pile of kickboards and saw with relief that my backpack was still safely stashed under them.

Before I knew it, Ronson and Falcon had pulled me out of the pool, and The Falcon was whacking me in the middle of my back, trying to get water out of my mouth.

I could hear Jessica nearby. "Oh, brother, what an infant. I mean, Ms. Falcon, we've got to have people on the team who can eggbeater without drowning. I mean, come *on*."

"Roger that, Captain Hale." The Falcon turned to me. "What happened, Peter? The whole reason I chose you for synchro was because you're not a completely terrible swimmer."

Thankfully, Jessica brought out the best in me, so I was prepared with my response.

"Honestly, Ms. Falcon, I just panicked. Jessica is so good at this, in fact she's so *amazing* at every single thing she does, that I find it pretty difficult to live up to those standards. And you know, I just kind of freaked out. I'm really, really sorry."

The Falcon scratched her chin and wrinkled her forehead.

"Hmm. A refreshingly honest response. Peter, there are 'A' players in the world—people like Jessica and myself—and then there are people like you, the 'C' players. Sooner or later, you've just got to learn to deal with it, simple as that."

"You mean I've got to learn to get real, right, Ms. Falcon?"

Her face broke into a wide smile.

"That's the spirit, Peter." And she whacked me on the back one more time.

Jessica, however, was not stupid. Her eyebrows narrowed into a squint and her normally dazzling blue eyes suddenly seemed dark and evil.

In the sweetest, most innocent voice I could muster, I said, "Captain Hale, thank you so, so much for saving my life. I am proud to have someone of your ability leading our team."

She balled up her hands into fists, cracked her knuckles, and dove back into the water.

Apparently there's a rule that, when you almost drown, you must sit out of the rest of practice. So I just sat there by the side of the pool, making sure my backpack was okay and watching my friends and the rest of the synchro team being put through the paces by Super-Captain Hale.

Jessica looked like she was taking out on the rest of the team the anger she felt toward me. Gary did plenty of crying, Plumpy looked miserable, and every once in a while Izmir would shoot me a hateful look. But I didn't really care. Today I had a book to protect, and anyway, there would be plenty of horrible synchro practices for me in the future.

When The Falcon finally blew the whistle to end the water torture, I grabbed my backpack out of the kickboard pile and headed to the locker room. Plumpy and the guys sulked in, took one look at me, and kept on walking. Didn't matter. I dressed, packed, and got out of the boys' locker room as soon as possible. I waved to The Falcon at the other end of the pool, ignored whatever she said to me, and walked as fast as I could out of the pool complex.

As I pushed through the double doors, I collided with somebody on the other side, lost my balance, and tumbled backward for the third time that afternoon. My bag fell to the floor, so I quickly scrambled to my feet and grabbed it. When I looked up, I saw Jessica flaring her nostrils at me.

Well, of course. This couldn't be easy now, could it?

She poked her finger into my chest. "First you fake drown and now you run me over again? I don't know what kind of a game you think you're playing."

Jessica was no fool. I'd learned that much from our years of battles. Best to just tell her the truth.

I sighed. "Jessica, I guess you've found me out. Truth is, I've been in love with you since the first grade, and I'm trying to find all the different ways I can literally throw myself into your arms."

She balled up her fists, showed her teeth, and for a second she reminded me of a coiled snake, preparing to strike.

"Listen, freak, you better not mess with me. If I didn't have to go pound people in my mixed martial arts class right now, I'd stay here and break you into pieces with my own bare hands."

"I would have preferred 'I love you too, Peter,' but I understand. You've got to get used to the idea."

Jessica stomped her feet, and her face looked like it was about to explode. She bent down and grabbed her backpack, then walked across the pool deck and out the glass exit door to the outside parking lot. And I would have turned around and walked the other way, except that I noticed something that I guess I'd never noticed before.

Jessica Hale had the same color and type of backpack as I did. Man, with the same color backpack it would be so easy to—

Uh-oh. We'd both dropped our backpacks when we'd collided.

I ripped the bag off my back, unzipped it, and looked inside. There was no leather-bound book. All I saw were kitten notebooks, a copy of *Darcey Jones*, and pens with rainbow caps. I had Jessica's backpack. Which meant—

Jessica had my backpack. Jessica had The Book.

I looked through the huge glass window separating the swimming complex from the outside; Jessica was walking along a crushed rock path in the middle of the construction site toward the parking lot. I took off after her. Down the pool deck and out one of the exit doors. Jessica was now at the parking lot, opening up the back door of a light purple car.

"Jessica, wait!" I yelled.

But before she could hear me, the door closed, the car took off, and that's when I slipped.

CHAPTER NINE

MISS MARMALADE'S

"You okay, Peter?" I heard Plumpy yell from behind as I rolled over. He and the guys were running from the pool complex with the construction foreman, Eddie.

I licked mud off my lips, slipped and stumbled to my feet, then stepped up to the crushed rock path. "No, I'm not okay. Not even close."

Eddie looked at me and gave his head a little shake. "Got to be careful around here, it's a construction site, you know."

"Really?" I answered, more than a little annoyed. "Hard to tell with the dump trucks, bulldozers, and guys with shovels."

"Oh yeah, construction guys use that kind of stuff all the time."

I shook my head. Apparently Eddie wasn't used to sarcasm.

"What the heck happened, Peter? I heard you yell at Jessica and then sprint after her before you, well…"

Izmir started to laugh. "Before Peter went for a nose drive in the mud."

"It's nose *dive,* Izmir. Listen guys, I'm in deep doo-doo here."

The construction foreman jumped forward and moved his hand back and forth. "No you aren't. We never use manure this close to a school. Against building codes. That mud you fell into is a mixture of topsoil, clay, sand, and mulch." He pointed toward the tree line. "You'd have to go another hundred feet to reach the manure."

Between this guy and Izmir, my head was about to explode.

"I'm serious guys, I'm in trouble. I ran into Jessica on the pool deck, we both fell down, and then she accidentally grabbed my bag and took off. That's why I was running after her."

Plumpy looked at the bag around my shoulders and smiled. "Which means *you've* got *her* backpack?"

I nodded.

His face hardened. "So we can look through her stuff?"

I shook my head and swallowed hard. "I've got something important in my backpack. Something Jessica can't see."

"What is it?"

I had a problem. I knew I couldn't let that book get into Jessica's hands, but I also didn't know if I could trust the guys. At least not yet.

"It's—got my copy of *Darcey Jones* in there, and my mother will kill me if I'm unprepared for class again. Dorney called her last time."

Izmir grabbed Jessica's bag out of my hand, unzipped it, and pulled out Jessica's copy of *Darcey Jones.*

"Here, now you can be prepared."

Time was slipping away. I imagined Jessica finding The Book, going to the local police, my life ending before it had even really begun. Then I imagined the Bookbinding Brotherhood getting hunted down and destroyed, all because I was a moron who couldn't hold onto my bag for an hour.

I needed the guys' help.

"Guys, I can't tell you what's in that bag. But if you help me get it back… I'll show you."

"You're serious?" Plumpy said. "It's that important?"

"Completely-freaking-out-inside serious. I *have* to get that bag before Jessica looks inside it."

"But what if she's already looked inside it?"

I was panicking. "I have to get that bag."

Eddie stepped into our circle carrying a garden hose. "I can drive you over there, but first we need to clean you up." Eddie had a queer smile on his face as he blasted me with water.

A few minutes later I was in the back of his "Shadylady Construction" van, completely soaked, but at least free of mud. Izmir was just about done drying me off with a leaf blower when the van stopped on Main Street five minutes later.

I looked out the window at the familiar sign for Miss Marmalade's: an enormous picture of Delilah Marmalade herself. With curly brown hair, big shiny white teeth, long silver fingernails, and a beauty mole above her upper lip, she was beautiful in the same way that the sun was beautiful. You want to look at it, but if you do it for too long, you might just go blind.

Marmalade was a minor celebrity in our town, so I knew plenty about her. She won the femjitsu world championships when she just out of high school, and a few years later she hit it big with Fierce Pounders, her luxury clothing line. Then just a few years ago, she opened Miss Marmalade's Gym as her way to train the next generation of Fierce Pounders. Apparently that included Jessica Hale.

"So what's your plan?" Plumpy asked as I slid open the van door.

I inched over to the window, put my face carefully against the glass, and looked around. After a minute, I turned back to the guys.

"Okay, they're all bunched up in the middle practicing whatever it is they do. The book bags are hanging up against the outside walls. I'll go in first, sneak in around the outside. After a minute, I need you guys to come in and cause a distraction. That should give me the time I need to switch the bags and get out of there."

"What kind of distraction?" asked Plumpy.

"Beats me. Make a bunch of noise, act like idiots. You should be able to figure that out."

The guys looked unsure.

"Okay?"

Plumpy exchanged looks with Gary and Izmir.

"Okay," they said.

I pushed open the front door to Marmalade's quietly, cracking it only wide enough to slip through. Once inside, I took a deep breath and looked around. Marmalade's was, like its owner, a strange mixture of martial arts and high fashion. Mannequins lined the perimeter of the gym, each one doing a different kick or punch, each one wearing a different outfit—complete with sunglasses, purses, and high heels. Fifty or so girls stood in the center of the dojo, screaming and grunting while practicing their kicks, punches, and grappling moves. Meanwhile, Miss Marmalade herself barked out instructions from the front of the classroom, her purse swinging from her side. She wore skinny high heels and cracked an enormous whip.

I had entered from the rear of the room; the girls were mostly facing away, luckily. Along against the rear wall beside me, but at the other side of the room, I spotted the book bags, hung up in a row.

The sound of girls screaming, along with the weird smell combination of pungent perfume and sweaty kids, was enough to make me dizzy. I put my hands on my knees and took a couple of deep breaths. Then I looked back up.

A whip cracked loudly and the girls immediately stopped and came to attention. The place went quiet, and I jumped behind the nearest mannequin so nobody would see me. Peeking out, I watched Miss Marmalade walk through the maze of girls like she was inspecting them. Any second now, I thought, the guys should be making their distraction. My hope was the crowd of girls would run to the front, giving me the time I needed to switch the bags.

"Ladies, sometimes what's missing in life is the proper motivation. When I told everyone I was entering the Femjitsu World Championships at age nineteen, people told me I didn't have a chance. But I knew all I needed was the proper motivation. So guess what I did. I went two hundred—count 'em ladies, two hundred days—without ever wearing... anyone? *High heels*. Shocking, I know. But why, you ask? Because I told myself that when I won the worlds, I would go out and buy myself the most expensive pair of eight-inch Manolo Blahnik high heels I could find."

I looked back to the front door. Still no sign of the guys. It had been at least three minutes since I'd come into Marmalade's.

"The vision of those high heels drove me, and the next year I pounded that bad skin, bad hair, mismatched-outfit fool from the East Region. Then, as a reward, I bought myself not one pair, but *two*. Now, ladies, you might not be ready for a pair of Manolo Blahniks just yet—but a nice pair of Fierce Pounders might do the trick."

The guys weren't coming. I would have to do this on my own.

Marmalade ripped a white sheet off a table in the front, revealing a shiny pair of silver high heels with sparkles all over them.

The crowd of girls squealed with excitement.

"Ladies, I want your punches harder, your kicks higher, your single-leg takedowns faster. And each time you practice, picture yourself slipping these Fierce Pounders on.

"Now, are you ready to practice? On your punches, I want to hear you yell 'Fierce!' On your kicks, I want to hear 'Pounders!' Are you ready?

"Punch!" Miss Marmalade yelled.

"Fierce!" the class responded, lunged and punching air in unison.

"Kick!" Marmalade commanded.

"Pounders!" the class responded.

And on it went.

While the girls practiced, I stealthily made my way from mannequin to mannequin, until finally I was only a few feet from Jessica's bag—*my* bag, I mean. And I was just about to step behind the next mannequin when, all of a sudden, Miss Marmalade shouted out a brand new command.

"Reverse!"

At that, the entire class of girls jumped a full half-turn. And instead of me being in the rear of the class, behind the girls, I was now right in the front. I froze, held my breath, and stayed behind my mannequin, hoping nobody would see me.

They continued.

"Punch."

"Fierce."

"Kick."

"Pounders!"

And then I heard something different. A scream.

Marmalade commanded them to stop. "What is it?"

"Miss Marmalade. I think something's behind that mannequin."

I stiffened, trying to make myself as skinny and small as possible.

"I see it too, Miss Marmalade. You think it's an animal?"

"Probably another rat." Marmalade was speaking again. "Lizbeth, grab the flamethrower."

Flamethrower?

"Best to get rid of those critters once and for all."

CHAPTER TEN

THE PINK DRAGON

K nowing my skin was not fire resistant, I made one of the easier decisions of my life and stepped out from behind the mannequin.

A roomful of sweaty, fierce-pounding girls looked stunned—but only for a moment. They began growling and yelling as they advanced toward me. I held onto that mannequin like she and her high heels were my best friends.

Then I heard the loud crack of Marmalade's whip, and the girls stopped their advance and parted. Marmalade strutted through the pack, whip in one hand, flamethrower in the other. She winced when she saw me. She tilted her head and pointed a long painted nail at me, her whip dangling in front of her.

"That is truly the ugliest rat I have ever seen."

"That's not a rat, Miss Marmalade," a familiar voice said. "His name is Peter Mills, and he's a hideously annoying boy who goes to my school."

Up stepped Jessica Hale, wearing a pink femjitsu smock and a bright pink belt.

"So what is this Peter *creature* doing in my dojo?"

I sure could use that distraction right about now, I thought. I turned to look at the front door. No sign of the guys anywhere.

"Well, Miss Marmalade," I said. "It's sorta funny actually. Turns out Jessica and I have the same backpack, and she mistakenly grabbed mine after synchro practice, and I just came over here to switch them back. Decided to come in and do it quietly so I wouldn't interrupt you." I spun and grabbed for my backpack—but just as I reached for it, the crack of a whip sounded right next to my ear and the bag exploded away from my hand. It sounded—and felt—like a bomb had gone off in my ear. I wheeled around to find Marmalade and Jessica both smiling at me, their eyes all squinty.

"Are you referring to Miss Hale?"

"Ah… yes?"

"Then you will address her according to her dojo name: the Pink Dragon."

That actually seemed quite fitting.

"Okay, then. The Pink Dragon has my backpack, and I have hers."

"You have my backpack?" Jessica said.

"Technically you took my backpack and I just want to switch them back."

"You didn't go through my stuff, did you?"

"Wouldn't dream of it. So, I'll just give you back your bag, I'll take mine, and I can see myself out."

Marmalade cracked the whip again. "I don't think so."

"No, really," I stammered. "It would be no problem at all."

Marmalade cleared her throat. "*You*, a… a *boy*… comes into my dojo uninvited, and you think that's something I can forget?"

"Yes, ma'am," I said quickly. "In fact I was counting on it, and I thank you in advance for your understanding. Good day to you both." I made a slight bow, but as I tried to walk past Marmalade, she grabbed me with her pinky. I tried to move, but couldn't. She had immobilized me with a single, two-inch-long finger.

She eyed me like a cat inspecting its prey. "It just so happens that you might be a good training exercise for our girls here. A chance to go up against some live competition." She looked me over. "Well, almost live. Any of you girls want a shot at this boy?"

Uh-oh. That didn't sound good.

The girls all shouted at once, but Jessica turned around and cut them off with a wave of her hand. "This one's all mine, Miss Marmalade."

"Very well, Pink Dragon. Girls, prepare the Cage of Death."

The entire place erupted in screams, and the crowd of girls ran to the opposite side of the school. Two big girls grabbed me and dragged me over to the other side of the dojo, where an enormous heart-shaped platform was surrounded by a steel cage.

Before I knew it, the girls had ripped my coat and backpack off, and I was being thrust up the steps, through the metal gate, and into the Cage of Death.

Before I even had a chance to get my bearings, Jessica and Miss Marmalade followed me in.

"Wait, Miss Marmalade, I—"

Miss Marmalade motioned to one of the girls, who rang the bell, signaling us to begin.

Jessica screamed, then spun around and did some high kicks into the air. She settled back into a fighting stance.

"Bring it, Squishy!"

Having never been in a fight in my life, I had no idea how to "bring it." But I did know how to talk.

"N-n-no, *you* bring it."

Jessica shook her head.

"The Pink Dragon never makes the first move."

"Does the Pink Dragon always speak of herself in the third person?"

"Shut it, Peter. The longer this lasts, the worse I'll make this for you, I promise."

"And by 'this,' you obviously mean our budding romance, right?"

Jessica screamed, then burst at me like she'd been shot out of a cannon. I did the only thing I could think to do: I dove out of the way head-first.

As I fell to the floor, I felt her collide with my legs. I landed awkwardly, then scrambled to my feet as quickly as I could, spinning around to prepare for Jessica's next attack. But she was still picking herself up from the mat, a little bit of blood coming from her nose.

By some kind of miracle, I had managed to trip her.

I had hurt the Pink Dragon.

Jessica wiped the blood off with her hand, breath coming out of her nostrils like fire out of a dragon. A very *Pink* Dragon.

"You are *so* dead," she growled.

She came at me fast, and again I dove out of the way. But this time she anticipated my move, jumped over my tripping leg, and landed right on top of me. Her first punch missed, but her next fifty punches pretty well landed on target.

At some point, I think my face exploded, because things got dark, with little sparks flying around, and I was having some kind of dream. I dreamt about Marmalade's whip hitting my head and my face bursting into thousands of pairs of Manolo Blahnik high heels. The whole thing was strangely mesmerizing. And then, at some point, even the sparkly shoes went away.

And everything was black.

CHAPTER ELEVEN

INTO THE TREES

I awoke to something cold and wet.

I choked, coughed, then looked up at the giant shiny teeth of Miss Delilah Marmalade. She handed a bucket to one of her girls and laughed at me. "Wow, you really are sad and pathetic. Even for a boy."

A couple of girls dragged me out of the Cage of Death and were kind enough to let me drop the remaining three feet to the floor. When I regained the ability to breathe, I felt like what I imagine a watermelon must feel like after being mauled by a lion. A wave of nausea crashed over me, and I put my head between my legs. When that finally passed, I looked around, my field of vision still cloudy. But something on the floor just a few feet away jumped out at me: my bag, the one Jessica had taken. I crawled over, unzipped it, and peeked inside.

The Book… it was still there.

I slipped the bag over my shoulder, stumbled to my feet, and wobbled toward the gym's front door. Marmalade's next generation of Fierce Pounders parted and laughed, mocking me with every painful step. Finally, when I thought the humiliation couldn't get any worse, I felt warm breath on the back of my neck and heard a whispering voice: "Thought you'd put up more of a fight than that, Peter. I'm a little disappointed."

And that's when the chanting started. "Squishy, Squishy, Squishy, Squishy."

I walked as fast as my dizzy head and wobbly legs would allow. When at last I made it out of Marmalade's, I collapsed.

But someone was there to catch me. Plumpy, Gary, and Izmir held me up, and the looks on their faces pretty much told me that my face looked as bad as it felt.

"I thought you were going to help me," I managed to say.

The guys exchanged guilty looks.

"Well, thanks for nothing," I said, working up the strength to steady myself.

I shook free of the guys, put my head down, and started down Main Street, doing my best imitation of walking.

In case you've never had the pleasure of experiencing it, getting beat up hurts. A lot. My nose felt like a hundred tiny needles were poking it. Tears fell steadily from the inside corners of my eyes, and not because I was crying. I had a terrible headache. And I felt like I was going to throw up.

All while I was trying to walk away from my friends. The ones who'd abandoned me.

"Peter!" Plumpy yelled. "You're hurt and you need help. Come back here and Eddie will give you a ride home."

As hurt as I was, I was even more angry. The guys were supposed to have been my distraction. They were supposed to be my friends. They never showed.

Miraculously I found the energy and balance to speed up to a jog, but they kept following. Finally a wave of dizziness overwhelmed me, about twenty feet before I got to the new gourmet skim milk joint, Skim Shady's. I put my head between my knees once more.

"Stop being stupid, Peter, and get in the van," Izmir yelled.

Then I saw it from between my legs. An alley ran along one side of Skim Shady's, leading to the back of the store. And behind that? The woods.

I needed to be alone. And what better place than the woods, somewhere none of us were ever allowed to go?

I spun around, and somehow managed not to collapse again as I limp-jogged down the alley. The guys were yelling, but the farther I went, the quieter their voices became. When I reached the end of the alley, I looked around and, confident I was alone, I ran under the cover of the trees.

When I was little, I once accidentally ran into the woods behind my house. I only got a few feet into the trees before my dad snatched me back. He was so scared. He told me no one was allowed in the forest, and if Mom ever found out, we'd both be in big trouble. And so, all my life, I'd avoided the woods. Everybody did. Girls said the woods were dangerous. But as I walked amidst the trees today, the woods didn't look so dangerous to me.

In fact, they looked beautiful. Sunlight filtered through a canopy of leaves above me. Light shimmered off leaves that rustled in the breeze. I saw how many shades of green there really were.

The woods *sounded* incredible, too. A few birds and animals, and the background noise of rustling leaves, but other than that… *silence*. No girls squealing. No teachers telling me to read a dumb book. No mother having air-quote talks.

And then there was the smell. I couldn't place quite place it, so I took a long deep breath. No perfume, no pink bus exhaust, no hair product. It was an amazing, clean, pure smell: the smell of nothing but fresh air and trees.

These beautiful woods, this soothing silence and clean air… they affected me. I smiled. I smiled so big, the corners of my mouth stung, and it was only then I remembered that my nose felt like someone was standing on it and my brain felt like mud.

But for some strange reason, all of that was okay.

I walked slowly down a long hill and found a creek at the bottom. The water was a clear blue-gray except where it ran into the rocks and bubbled up into white foam. A fish darted through the water, then get lost in a tree branch that extended into the water from the bank.

I knelt down beside the creek and dipped my hand in. The water was cool—much colder than I would have guessed. I cupped some in my hands and drank. Amazing.

I splashed the cool water on my face. More pain, more needles in my face, and the water on my hands turned a shade of pink from the blood still trickling from my nose.

I followed the creek for a few minutes, eventually reaching a spot where a large tree had fallen across the creek, its top branches reaching to the other side. It hovered there about five or six feet above the water, with green moss growing on its bark.

I cocked my head and studied that tree. If you used your imagination, I thought, it could be a bridge. I immediately scrambled up the roots, onto the trunk, and crawled slowly across.

The trees were thicker on the other side of the creek. I had to keep my forearm in front of me to keep the smaller branches out of my face. And then, after a couple minutes of this, all of a sudden the trees weren't so thick. Several of them lay on the ground—fallen, or maybe someone had cut them down. But whatever the cause, the effect was a little clearing in the middle of the forest. My own private room in the middle of all these trees.

I sat down on one of the logs. It was time to figure out exactly what I had sacrificed my face to protect.

I took the big grey cloth bundle out of my bag, unwrapped it, and held The Book in my hands. It was bigger than our textbooks, twice as thick, and heavy. I traced my finger in the three carved letters, just like I'd done in front of Drummond.

I had just grabbed the cover to flip it open when a tree branch snapped.

I went rigid, listening.

And then I knew I wasn't alone.

There were voices.

CHAPTER TWELVE

THE BOOK REVELATION

I was running through the trees, away from the clearing, when I heard the voices again.

"Peter! Peter, where are you?"

Unbelievable. They followed me. Though I was still angry with them, a part of me was glad they came, so I walked back. When I reached the clearing, the guys were all there. Plumpy looked concerned, Izmir looked grumpy, and Gary looked scared.

"Peter! Thank goodness you're okay," Plumpy said.

"Have you actually *looked* at my face? I'm not sure this qualifies as 'okay.' You *abandoned* me back there."

"I know. I'm sorry," Plumpy said.

"Me too," Gary said, his lip trembling, his eyes darting around the forest like he thought a monster was lurking in the shadows.

Izmir just stood there, stone-faced.

"And you, Izmir?" Plumpy asked.

"And me what?" Izmir asked.

Plumpy punched him in the arm. "Why don't you tell Peter how sorry you are?"

"Because I'm not. *He's* the idiot who went into Marmalade's in the first place."

"Izmir," Plumpy growled.

Izmir rolled his eyes. "Fine. Me. Sorry."

Big step for Izmir.

"Peter, can we get out of here now? Gary's so scared I think he's going to pee his pants."

"I am not," Gary whimpered. "I haven't peed my pants in weeks."

"The forest is giving him the creeps. And if we get caught, we're all dead."

I laughed. "And who's going to catch us? Did you notice the complete absence of human beings in here?"

"But you know the rules, Peter. People aren't allowed in the woods."

"And thus, the perfect place to hide."

"Whatever. Let's just get out of here, okay?" Plumpy's eyes darted about. Looked like Gary wasn't the only one getting the creeps from this place.

"You guys go on," I said. "You said you were sorry, and I accept your apology. Now go home. I've got things to do."

"Here?"

"Yes, here."

"What's in that bag that's so important?"

"I said I'd show you what's in the bag after you helped me get it back. And I don't consider watching me get my face beat in 'helping.'"

"It may not be worth much," Plumpy explained, "but it wasn't much fun watching you get beat up."

"You're right. That's not worth much."

Plumpy shook his head at me, then turned and put his arms around Gary and Izmir. They huddled together for a moment, whispering, and then Plumpy turned back.

"We'd like to stay with you."

"No, I really don't," Gary said.

"Shut it, Gary," said Izmir, arms folded across his chest.

"We know we didn't help you back there, and we're sorry," Plumpy said. "But we're your friends—and we want to stay."

"And you want to see what's in the bag." I said.

"Yeah."

I'll admit, I hadn't really thought this through. Drummond had watched me for years before deciding I was ready, and even then, he gave me a choice. And yet, after all that, I was still freaking out.

Would my friends be ready for this?

Then I remembered something Drummond said. "Binders aren't very good at changing things, Peter. We need a *changer*. We need *you*."

I sat down on one of the fallen logs, unzipped my bag, and took out The Book.

The guys gathered around.

"A book?" Plumpy observed.

"I think it's a very different kind of book."

"You mean you don't know?" Plumpy asked.

I shook my head.

"Well, there's no skirts," Izmir pointed out.

"Or horses," Gary added.

I tapped the cover. "These letters: B, A, M. They stand for something. *Be. A. Man.*"

That surprised them. Plumpy rubbed his finger against his lips. Izmir looked annoyed.

"Is it a cookbook or something?" Gary asked.

"Or something. Mr. Drummond, the bookbinder, gave it to me."

"Bad Breath Drummond?" Izmir asked.

"Peter," said Plumpy. "What the heck is going on here?"

"Honestly, I'm not sure."

"Then start with what you know."

So I told them about the note in the locker, the blue message in the diet book, the disaster with Jessica and Dr. Branless in the bathroom, and, finally, the meeting with Drummond.

By the time I was finished, Plumpy's forehead was scrunched up and wrinkled. "And you swear you're not messing with us?"

"No way."

I described the weird artifacts in Drummond's secret cave, then described the old photo of the army. The *man* army.

"And Izmir, the name of that army was—" I hesitated and braced myself. "The Ottoman Turkish Empire."

Izmir's mouth fell open, then he shook his head like he was clearing it. He leaned toward me and grabbed my shoulders. "Did you just say *Turkish*?"

I nodded.

He took a deep breath and then stood up. "The Ottoman Turkish Empire," he whispered to himself. Then a look of concern crossed his face and he bent down.

"But Peter, did they look—"

"Yes, Izmir, they looked like you. Just like you."

A smile crossed his face and he laughed. He stood up straight and spun around. "And they looked mighty?"

"Yes."

"And huge?"

"Yep."

Izmir sat down, and his eyes glazed over like he was in a trance.

"So Peter," Plumpy said, scratching his chin. "We've got a huge man army, a picture of a bunch of men in suits, and an old document signed by nothing but men."

"And we've got this book. *Be A Man.*"

"So what's it all mean?" Plumpy asked.

I supposed Drummond was right: maybe I *had* always known. Well, maybe not *known* known. But I'd known that something wasn't right. And now it was time to say it out loud.

"I think it means that girls, well… they haven't always been in charge."

CHAPTER THIRTEEN

FOLLOWING DIRECTIONS

We sat there in stunned silence—processing what I'd said, what it meant. Gary tried to be brave, but after a couple of minutes I guess he couldn't take it anymore: he jumped up and ran screaming into the woods. Izmir had to chase him down, throw him over his shoulder, and carry him back to the clearing.

That's when Plumpy spoke up.

"It does explain a lot."

"Yeah," Izmir said, breaking a stick in half. "It does."

"Drummond told me to read this book and use it to change things," I said.

Plumpy edged closer to me. "Have you looked inside?"

"Not yet. I say we do it together."

The four of us grabbed the cover and opened it up.

"Whoa," said Gary, as we all stared at the first page. "What *is* this?"

The page was a combination of dotted lines and numbers. I wondered if it might be another language.

Plumpy squinted at the page. "Looks like a diagram, and directions to build something."

"Build what?" asked Gary.

Plumpy squinted some more. "I have no idea, but I say we follow these directions. *Step One: take a regular piece of paper and fold it in half.*" Plumpy looked at me and I shrugged. Then I reached into my bag, tore some sheets out of my notebook, and handed them out. Each of us folded a piece of paper in half, just like the directions said.

"What's next?" asked Plumpy, who was now studying his own folded piece of paper.

I read step two, then looked up.

"Anybody need me to repeat that?" Apparently nobody did.

We worked like this through the rest of the steps until, a few minutes later, we were almost done.

"*Step Ten,*" I read. "*Grab your paper from the bottom so that the wide side is facing the sky and the pointy end is facing away from your body. Then cock your arm back and, with a smooth motion, bring your arm forward and slightly upward. At the last moment, release your paper.*"

This was totally weird. I looked at the others, and could tell by their faces that they thought so too.

"How about we all do it at the same time," Gary said.

"Sounds good," Izmir said.

"Okay then," I said. "Ready… set…"

"Wait, wait, wait," Gary interrupted. "Do we cock our arm back first, or at the very end?"

"Cock it back first, like this," Plumpy said.

"Okay, got it."

I started again. "Ready… set… go!"

Together, we let go of our papers—and the most incredible thing happened. They all started to soar through the air, like they were… like they were…

"Airplanes!" Plumpy shouted, his index finger high in the air. "We just made *airplanes*! Can you believe it?"

Airplanes were those enormous, metal, jet-powered flying machines women traveled on for long trips out of the region. Had we really just *built* airplanes, in a few minutes, out of nothing but paper? No, I couldn't believe it. But there was no denying that that's exactly what they were: paper airplanes.

Gary grabbed his plane from where it landed, and launched it again. This time it did a loop before returning to the ground and crashing. Izmir grabbed his and launched it high into the air. It took a sharp turn to the left and hit the branch of a tree before spiraling down to the ground. Plumpy just held his in his hands, about three inches from his face, examining it closely. I found my plane stuck into a crack on the ground. I noticed the pointy end was crinkly like an accordion. Without even thinking, I straightened the nose out and threw it again. It went straight, with no turns or loops, then descended slowly until it landed smoothly on the ground.

For the next thirty minutes we didn't talk. We just grabbed paper out of our bags and made a couple dozen more airplanes. We threw them into the air, fixed them after they crashed, and made more planes. The whole thing felt so natural, like we'd been doing this our whole lives.

Finally Plumpy looked at his watch. "Yikes," he said. "I'm late."

I stuffed The Book back in my bag, and we ran out of the woods as fast as we could, walking carefully down the back alley at Skim Shady's so nobody would see us. Then we jogged down Main Street toward the area of town where we all lived. Somehow the excitement of everything had acted to dull the pain I should have been feeling in my face.

When we finally reached the part of the neighborhood where we needed to split up, Izmir grabbed me by the shoulders, squeezed, and shook me violently. Then he ran away, screaming "Ottoman Turkish Empire!" into the air.

I was going to be late for dinner. Mom would yell at me. She'd also freak at my mangled face. And of course, I actually *had* a mangled face, which at any minute would start hurting really bad. But I didn't care.

I had just spent the afternoon in the woods with my friends, making paper airplanes from instructions we found in a secret book about how to really be a man. At that moment, all I felt was happiness. And maybe something else; something I had never felt before in my life.

Hope.

CHAPTER FOURTEEN

RUBBER AND GLUE

When I woke the next morning, I could hardly see out of my left eye, my cheek was puffed up like a balloon, and my nose felt like it was stuffed full of thumbtacks. I looked in the bathroom mirror and an ugly twelve-year-old with a black and blue face stared back at me. The Pink Dragon did impressive work.

I walked to school wearing a hooded sweatshirt and sunglasses, and prepared my version of how my eyes and nose had come to look like scrambled blue cheese. After debating a few options—some gruesome, some comical, some heroic—I finally settled on my story: that I had miraculously saved my poor dad's life by pulling a refrigerator off of him using nothing but my face. But as soon as I climbed the stairs of our school, I saw a flier taped to the school's front door, and my heart sank.

Peter 'Squishy' Mills Gets Face Bashed by the Incomparable Jessica Hale

So much for my side of the story.

And so I endured an entire day of humiliation, highlighted by Mrs. Dorney, who said what an honor it must have been to get beaten up by someone as beautiful and talented as Jessica Hale.

Really?

After school, I was trudging over to the pool for day two of trying to get my one-piece on, when Jessica burst out of the girls' locker room and stopped me. At the same time, The Falcon walked by us on her way to yell at some of the construction workers, who were installing new ceiling tiles.

"Why hello, Ms. Falcon, delightful to see you," said Jessica. "I hope we've got a challenging practice for today."

"Oh, Jessica, you kill me. Practice will be as hard as you want it to be, because you're in charge!" The Falcon shook her head and laughed.

Jessica turned and stepped toward me. Practically stood on my toes.

"Well, well, Peter. You know, black and blue all over is a good color for your face. Looks like you've got ugly makeup on. Not that you needed it. You do ugly just fine."

Jessica Hale's smug smile. I wanted to wipe it off her perfect little face. But based on what happened at Miss Marmalade's, I knew I couldn't actually do that. At the very least I would have liked to have verbally assaulted her with an embarrassing comment or two. But at the moment... I had nothing. So in addition to beating me up in front of a room full of girls, she had bested me with her putdown. Ugly makeup. I would need to remember that one.

At least I had better luck getting into my one-piece swimsuit. Only took me three tries before I got both feet in the correct holes. But practice itself was another matter. Synchronized swimming practice was the hardest thing I had ever done in my life. In addition to sculls and eggbeaters, today Jessica taught us how to do back layouts and front layouts, sailboats, bent knees, ballet legs, flamingos, verticals, cranes, knights, and fishtails.

But no matter how much my arms and legs hurt, without a doubt the most challenging part of the entire practice was keeping a smile on my beaten-up face. Allowing Jessica to use my face as a punching bag had given her enough pleasure already. I wasn't about to give her any more.

When at last The Falcon blew the whistle signaling the end of practice, I barely climbed out of the water before collapsing. I lay on my belly on the side of the pool, just thankful that it would be another twenty-three hours before I'd have to go through it all again. I couldn't imagine why anybody would ever voluntarily decide to do this sport for fun.

The guys and I limped out of practice together. I'm sure if you'd seen us, we would have looked like a group of old men on ice skates. We wobbled our way down to Main Street, then took it as far as Skim Shady's. We looked around to make sure nobody was watching, then we squeezed down the alley, out the back, and hobbled into the woods.

Walking through the woods seemed to revive us. I think it was all that clean air. Or maybe it was just the freedom. But anyways, I didn't notice the soreness so much anymore, and before I knew it we had reached the clearing. Which was good, because we had important work in front of us.

"Guys, I'm afraid I didn't get very far in The Book last night. I was pretty tired."

"Maybe it was all the blood you lost," suggested Plumpy. "The average twelve-year-old only has eight pints of blood. If you lost a pint through your face, I'm sure your body needed to shut down in order to make new blood."

"How do you know all that? You've slept through the last two hundred days of school."

Plumpy shrugged.

I continued. "Anyways, I saw something awesome in The Book last night, and I found the supplies we need in my dad's craft room." I opened up my bag and laid out a few items. "Any idea what I have here?"

Gary picked up something long, wide, thin, and pink. "Feels like rubber."

Izmir pointed to the other two items. "And you've got scissors and glue."

"Yep, separately that's all they are. But when you combine them together in just the right way, you have the perfect anti-Pink Dragon weapon."

I could tell by the looks on the guys' faces that they were hooked. I dumped out my bag, and more glue, scissors, and pink rubber sheets fell to the ground.

"Guys, all our lives we've let the Jessica Hales of the world to do all the punching. Well no more. On behalf of my face, and boys everywhere, I say it's time to punch back."

CHAPTER FIFTEEN

OPERATION PUNCH BACK

The next day at lunch, we grabbed our French-bean-and-mango salads and hustled to our normal spot. The first thing we did was eat—without counting. We didn't need The Falcon bothering us for failure to eat our lunch. The second thing we did was scope out the lunchroom—make sure we knew where everybody was sitting.

Specifically, where Jessica was sitting.

We laid a napkin between us, and Plumpy drew a quick map of the lunchroom. At the center, he made a red X, right where the Ice Princess was perched upon her throne.

Now it was my turn. I lowered my voice to a whisper and went over the plan. A simple plan, really, but one that required precision timing. I used my pen to go over it again and again. Finally Gary spoke up. As usual, he was shivering.

"Peter, I want to deliver the package."

I exchanged confused looks with Plumpy and Izmir.

"What are you talking about, Gary? You're the lookout."

"I-I'm the best one for the job. Plumpy isn't fast enough."

"And you are?"

Gary leaned forward even more. "I've been stealing peanuts out of my mom's purse for years. I'm quick with my hands. I can do this."

His shivers wouldn't stop, I could hear his knees knocking together under the table, and I could have sworn I saw his brown teddy bear stuffed down his pants.

"Gary, no offense, but you look nervous just talking about it. If you get caught, we're all dead."

Gary's gaze fell to the floor as I continued going over the plan. Then his head snapped back up.

"Guys, there's a lot I can't do. But this I *can* do. And I can do it better than any of you."

I wasn't so sure, and the other guys looked equally doubtful.

Gary's jaw tensed up and his body straightened out. "I promise." For once, his shivers were gone.

Plumpy patted him on the back. "Gary's right. He can do this. He deserves a shot."

Izmir just shrugged.

Gary's hands were folded, and his eyes stared into mine. It was probably not a very smart thing to send Gary in there, but I figured Plumpy was right: Gary did deserve a chance.

"Okay then, Gary. You're the bag man. That means Plumpy is on lookout. I'm still the main diversion, and Izmir will keep The Falcon occupied."

We all knew that timing this operation right would be critical. I looked at the clock. Three minutes until the lunch bell, and Jessica was still at her table.

And so it began.

Plumpy opened up his history textbook, and Gary grabbed something out of it and turned around. Izmir spotted The Falcon and stood up to walk near her. I grabbed my tray and walked over to the trash receptacles, just about fifteen feet from Jessica's table. To one side of me I saw Izmir make contact with The Falcon, and to the other side I noticed Gary getting into position among a group of kids that were walking back from their tables. So far, so good.

Our simple plan relied on three things.

First, that I would be able to utterly humiliate myself in front of the school. *Check.*

Second, that Jessica Hale would be her usual cruel and miserable self. *Check.*

And third, that Gary would be able to pull this off. *Oh, please please please.*

I took one last look at Gary, and he gave me the most imperceptible nod of the head in history. He was ready. And then I took one look at Jessica, she caught my eye, and—

I tripped. Big time.

I intentionally caught my feet together, launched my tray straight into the air, and landed on the floor, rolling over several times while my plate, fork, spoon, and cup fell from the sky toward me. I covered my face as the contents of my tray crashed around me. When I finally opened my eyes and moved my hands, I glanced toward Jessica's table. She was momentarily stunned. The rest of the cafeteria had joined her in silence.

And then the dam broke loose.

All at once, the girls in the cafeteria exploded in laughter. From her throne, Jessica led choruses of "dork" and "loser." And then she did something she just couldn't help: she acted like herself. She stood, balled up her fists, and rubbed them into her eyes.

"Oh, wittle Squishy fall down! Wow Peter, you're such a freak. First I have to save you from drowning, then I rearrange your face, and now you can't even walk? What a total loser."

The cafeteria erupted in girl laughter again.

Jessica stuck an L up to her forehead, and the rest of the girls at her table quickly followed. I endured it all with my cheek pressed against the cold cafeteria floor. Mango bits that had hit my face were now leaking into my mouth. And then, just as Jessica was high-fiving one of the girls at her table, I saw a blur behind her. Jessica took one last look around the cafeteria, soaking up the glory that comes from having just humiliated a fellow student.

And then she sat down.

The world seemed to move in slow motion. Jessica Hale, the Ice Princess herself, sat down, smiling and grinning. I could read her lips, saying "total loser" to someone across from her.

And when she hit her chair—

The world's loudest fart noise exploded from her butt.

There was an eerie awkward pause as Jessica screamed and looked around, frightened at what had happened. And then, yet again, the entire cafeteria exploded in laughter—but not just girl laughter this time. Boys joined in. And the eyeballs were no longer on me. Nope, I scrambled to my knees, grabbed my stuff, put it back on my tray, and quickly moved away without anyone so much as noticing me.

Because every other person in the cafeteria was focused entirely on Jessica Hale.

It's not every day the prettiest and most popular girl at school lets out a lunchroom fart that sounds like an exploding tuba. Jessica's face turned bright red as she stood back up to look at her chair. But there was nothing on her chair. And as she looked, the cafeteria exploded in laughter yet again. The boys were laughing even harder now.

And then the Ice Princess realized why they were all still laughing so loud. Something big, bright, and pink was stuck to her butt. She grabbed it with her hands and yanked as hard as she could, but it was no use: it just wouldn't come off. She looked around frantically for someplace to hide, her face increasingly desperate, then finally she grabbed her books and ran out of the cafeteria. I could hear her screaming all the way down the hall.

And then the bell rang. Right on time.

The kids in the cafeteria stood up, still laughing, probably trying to figure out what had just happened to the most popular girl in school. At the same time, Izmir, Plumpy, Gary and I disappeared into the crowd and moved down the hall to our next class. Nobody paid us any attention.

Izmir punched Gary in the arm and Plumpy messed up his hair.

"Gary, that was unbelievable," I said.

"Really? You don't think anybody saw me?"

"Not a chance," Plumpy said. "You were practically invisible."

Gary straightened up. "That sure was the loudest fart I've ever heard."

"The look on Jessica's face was priceless," Plumpy said.

"I would do anything to see that look again," said Izmir.

"Good," I laughed. "Because The Book's got tons more pranks."

"Tons?" Gary asked.

"Yep," I said. "Enough to keep us busy all year."

CHAPTER SIXTEEN

ONE SMALL STINK FOR MAN

The whoopee cushion incident made Jessica insanely grumpy, and the next day she took it out on us with another brutal synchro practice. Afterward, we limped out of the swimming complex and felt the heat of a warm spring day.

"Guys, this weather is perfect for our next prank."

Back at the clearing, I unzipped my bag and took out four plastic zip-lock bags and a couple of my dad's sewing needles. Plumpy pulled a small carton of eggs out of his bag.

"So, are you going to tell us what this is all about?" Plumpy asked.

"Kind of like a science experiment, Plumpy. You should like this."

I grabbed a sewing needle and made a hole in one of the eggs. Then I put the egg inside the bag and zipped it shut.

"According to The Book, the hole lets air gets into the egg, and the combination of the air and the heat causes the egg to rot. And when the egg rots…"

"It stinks," said Plumpy.

"Exactly."

We mapped out our plan, poked holes in the other three eggs, and sealed them shut. Plumpy agreed to keep them in his back yard all weekend.

"Don't worry," he said. "I won't let anything happen to them."

On Monday morning he met us outside school, handed us each a baggy with an egg, and reminded us to not open them until we'd made the drop. Then he yawned.

"Plumps, you didn't stay up all night watching the eggs, did you?" I said.

He yawned yet again. "You think I would stay up all weekend just so I could see a bunch of girls scream because of a stink bomb?"

"Absolutely."

Plumpy grinned. "Yeah, I did. Like you said, science experiment."

We agreed that since Gary had been so smooth at slipping the whoopee cushion under Jessica's bum, he'd earned another starring role in this next mission. The plan called for Gary to loosen the first two vents while walking to his first period class. He would loosen vents three and four heading to his second period class. And on the way to his third period class, at exactly 10:07 a.m., when the halls were completely packed with kids, he would turn off the lights to the building. The school really shouldn't have put the light switches where just anybody could get to them.

After second period, we headed out of the classroom and split up. After passing by the girls lounge, I saw my vent and slowed down. The big clock in the hall read 10:06. I unzipped my backpack, stuck my hand inside and grabbed my egg, safe inside its zip-lock bag. Gary had told us how to practice the move at home, and I'd gone over it a dozen or so times to make sure I had it down.

I looked up at the big clock in the hallway then glanced again at my vent. The top right screw of the vent was loosened and out just a bit, just like we'd discussed. I was in position.

The clock read 10:06 and fifty-two seconds. I took a deep breath, made sure I was ready to move quickly. Fifty-seven seconds. Fifty-eight. Fifty-nine.

10:07.

The school went dark and the kids went nuts. Gary had struck again.

I pulled the baggy out, lifted the edge of the vent back, then opened up the bag and dropped the egg down the vent, all in one fluid motion, just as I'd practiced. A moment later, I heard the egg go splat somewhere in the ductwork below the floor. An initial burst of stink rushed up, and some girl near me yelled, "Nasty! Tell Ernie to use the bathroom next time!"

I quickly tightened the screw back up, kept moving, and maybe ten seconds later, the lights to the building turned back on and the screaming died down. I looked up at the clock. The time was 10:07 and thirty-two seconds. Not bad. Not bad at all.

I turned and headed for my third period class, a class that all four of us shared. Izmir and Plumpy both nodded at me. We sat down, pulled out our books, and prepared for class. Gary walked in last and gave me a knowing smile. At 10:10 a.m., the bell rang.

Ms. Higgins had only just started her lecture about the benefits of phyto-nutrients for clean and beautiful skin when the smell hit our classroom. Heads turned as kids sniffed at the air.

Ms. Higgins wrinkled her nose, then walked to the door and opened it. As soon as she did, the rotten egg stink blasted into the room. Girls screamed and covered their noses.

I've got to admit: even for us boys, that was one *putrid* smell.

Higgins fell to her knees, gagging. The class ran over and around her, then pushed through the classroom door like sand squeezing through an hourglass. Problem was, in the hallway, the stink was even worse. Kids screamed and gagged while sprinting down the hallway for the exit doors.

We stood outside for the next hour, while Principal Lemming tried to get a handle on what kind of toxic smell was violating her school's air space. At one point, two big green trucks arrived and men wearing gas masks climbed out and headed inside the school. Ten minutes later, one of the gas mask guys came back out and talked to Principal Lemming. From fifty feet away I could see her react to whatever was being said like she was in pain. Then she grabbed a megaphone from The Falcon and stepped on top of a nearby bench. I'll never, ever forget the words that came out of her mouth.

"Students, may I have your attention please. Because of a mysterious gas leak, Finley Junior High will be closed for the rest of the day so the problem can be fixed."

A few seconds passed before we realized what that meant. Then all of a sudden, Plumpy started clapping. I looked at him and he shrugged. Izmir and I joined him, and then I saw Ernie Pile start to clap, but he kept missing his hands, then finally Gary, and then the rest of the guys on the quad joined in too. One of the guys began screaming, and then the cheers started. I'd never seen anything like it.

For real. I'd never in my life seen guys cheer about anything.

The girls stared at us like we were from outer space. They remained quiet in what Plumpy later called a "collective state of bewilderment." A few girls cried while others hugged. Lemming hopped back onto the bench and announced that the school would provide grief counselors for anybody having trouble processing the day's tragic events.

The gang and I decided we would do our grief counseling in the woods that day. We reviewed Operation Stink Bomb—and by "review" I mean we laughed for twenty minutes straight. With one well-executed prank, we had done something disgusting, funny, and *good* for the boys of Finley Junior High. Just like Drummond had ordered me to do, I was finally changing things.

CHAPTER SEVENTEEN

LOCKER CONFUSION

The Book was full of pranks. Sure, there was other stuff in The Book, but it all looked boring, so I did what I had learned to do my whole life: skip the boring parts. And the pranks were so much fun. In fact, I couldn't believe boys used to have this much fun before girls took over. Whenever I learned something new, I immediately shared it with the guys, and over the next month our lives fell into a simple routine of school, synchro, and pranks.

There was the day Mrs. Dorney rushed into class freaking out because there was blood all over her hands. If she had only licked her palms, she would've realized the blood tasted pretty good. Gary had squirted a packet of ketchup all over the doorknob just before Dorney reached class.

Then there was the day when three of Jessica's friends sloshed into the lunchroom with shoes and socks that were completely drenched. They didn't look happy, but *we* were thrilled. Izmir and Plumpy had filled a couple of trash cans with water, and Gary and I had leaned them up against the doors of the girls' restroom.

And there was the day of the school assembly. Principal Lemming stepped up to the wooden podium, placed her hands on the sides of it, and—the entire thing collapsed into a dozen pieces. Lemming fell down and rolled off the stage right into The Falcon's lap. The day before we had found a saw in the janitor's office and had cut the podium into exactly twelve different pieces, which we carefully put back together with scotch tape. And for a special touch, we carved into one of the pieces: *Jessica Hale Rocks!*

There were plenty of other pranks. The Book had tons of ways to create raunchy smells, make disgusting noises, and cause things to fall apart. Our objective was to cause as much mayhem or humiliation as possible.

And whenever we could, we'd also leave a little hint as to who might really be responsible for all these pranks: namely, none other than her worshipfulness herself, the Ice Princess of the sixth grade, Miss Pain-in-the-Butt Perfect, Jessica Hale.

And that brings us to the locker prank.

Finley had five hundred students, and five hundred lockers for those students. Each locker was protected by a combination lock, and it was up to each student to remember the combination to their own lock. But sometimes a kid would forget their combination; and at other times, occasionally, the school would need to look inside a kid's locker on their own. So for those special situations, Mr.

Ronson, the janitor, had a master key, a tiny little key, which could open all of the combination locks.

It was common knowledge that Ronson took naps in his office; you could walk by Ronson's office each afternoon and hear him sawing logs. What *wasn't* common knowledge was that Ronson was an extremely sound sleeper; Plumpy and I discovered this by accident one day. We'd gone into his office to ask him a question, we even spoke to him, right to his face, and incredibly, the guy never woke up. And when we noticed that Mr. Ronson left the keys for the school on his desk... well, that's when we came up with an awesome idea for a prank.

On the day of the locker prank, Gary slipped into the janitor's office and stole two keys while Ronson slept. One big key, one little. Then Gary stepped back outside into the hallway, blending in with the traffic of kids walking to their next class.

We chose this particular day for the prank because after school, all of the school staff were supposed to go to a big fancy meeting downtown for the Regional School Network. That meant the school would be empty—and, of course, locked.

Locked to anybody who didn't have a big key.

Our idea was elegant. A simple plan resulting in maximum mayhem. But it took several hours of hard work to pull it off. And when we were finished, we threw away that little key.

The next morning, I walked up the steps to our school and saw yet another paper flyer on the front door. This time, it was a drawing of a stick figure, a girl standing on top of other students, like she was squashing them with her feet and enjoying it. And across the top of the paper were the words "*Jessica Hale, Queen of Finley Junior High.*"

Who knew Izmir was such a good artist?

Then I opened the door and walked into school—and witnessed something I'd never seen before:

Hundreds of girls were fighting their lockers.

I'm not sure I've ever enjoyed strolling through school as much as I did that morning. So much hostility, by so many girls, was directed at these little tiny locks that just wouldn't open. On one side of the hall I saw a pair of girls yell "Fierce Pounders!" and then unload on their lockers with a flurry of punches and kicks. On the other side, one of Jessica's friends had pulled a fire extinguisher off the wall and was using it to beat her locker to death. The Falcon came by and grabbed the girl and pulled her away, but the girl was flipping out, screaming, "I've got homework I haven't finished!"

And what were the boys doing during all this? From what I could see, a whole lot of nothing. Sitting with their backs to their lockers. Sleeping. Watching the girls. But no anger. No femjitsu moves against metal locker doors. The boys appeared to be enjoying this.

Then whispers started to pass through the hall. Heads turned like dominoes. People were looking at the entrance doors. Looking at who just got to school. I'd have known that cocky walk, those cute legs, and those silver designer sunglasses anywhere.

Jessica Hale was in the building.

She sauntered down the hallway, her designer purse swinging over one arm, her other arm free to punch anybody who dared get in her way. When she saw her usual group of friends, she lifted her sunglasses up onto her forehead. "Hello, ladies. What's going on?"

But these girls weren't in the mood. They all stared back at her, hands on hips, steam coming out of their noses.

"Whatever. Looks like somebody didn't sleep very well last night." Jessica knocked over some boy as she blew through the crowded hallway to her locker. She spotted something above her locker and tore it off the wall. It was one of those "Jessica Hale, Queen" posters. She spun around. "Now this... this is hilarious! And so true. Who put it here?"

One of the girls squinted at Jessica. "As if you don't know?"

Now Jessica's face hardened. The smile was gone. "Why don't you lay off the two percent milk, Betsy? Not only does it put you in a bad mood, it makes you look like a buffalo in that skirt."

Jessica turned back around and started spinning through her combination lock. I held my breath; this was the moment of truth.

Jessica's lock opened with a click.

The entire school gasped behind her.

You see, of the five hundred students at Finley, only Jessica Hale was able to open her locker that morning.

She grabbed her books and turned back around, still clueless about what was happening. A huge group of girls gathered in a half circle around her.

Jessica ran her hand through her hair, and her face exploded into a smile. "I know, my hair totally has some extra pop this morning, don't you think? My mom's shipped in some Clydesdale hair product from out east. Stuff is incredible!"

One of Jessica's closest friends stepped out of the half circle and walked right up to the Ice Princess. "So, you find this all hilarious, do you? Not one of us can open our locker today. Nobody except you. Satisfied, *Queen* Jessica?"

"I'm sure I have no idea what you're talking about."

"Oh, I bet. Come on, ladies."

And with that, the horde of girls turned away from the Ice Princess and walked away. Which left Jessica in an unfamiliar spot: alone. But only for a moment. Within seconds, Principal Lemming walked up to her holding the "Queen of Finley" poster.

"Miss Hale, you and I need to have a talk."

And then Jessica was escorted away, doing the walk of shame toward the principal's office for the first time in her entire life.

And that wasn't the only good news. The rest of us went to our classes without books that day, and as a result, not much got done. The teachers and the girls were so rattled by the locker craziness that they didn't know how to function. But us boys were used to functioning at an extremely low level—so for us, this was perfect. In fact, if school had a lot more of nothing, I thought, I could get used to it.

CHAPTER EIGHTEEN

THE NAME

After the massive success of the locker prank, we knew we needed to come up with a name for our group, and we agreed to meet the following Saturday morning to brainstorm. So on Friday night, I went through The Book, looking for name ideas, when I noticed a couple of pages stuck together. I carefully peeled them apart—and couldn't believe what I'd found.

The next morning, as we sat in the clearing, I could hardly control my excitement.

"Anybody think of a good name for our group?" I asked.

Gary shrugged. "I think mine's pretty good."

For the record, Gary was terrible at this kind of thing. But I figured, who knows—maybe his newfound confidence was helping him in other areas of his life.

Gary cleared his throat. "The Four Boys In The Woods... Group." He paused and looked at each one of us. Izmir muttered something in Turkish, while Plumpy and I did the best we could to fake smile.

"That's a good start, Gary," I said. "Plumpy, what did you come up with?"

"Okay, well, you know how all of us are boys, but what we're doing is kind of unusual?"

"Yeah?"

Plumpy lifted his finger in the air. "I think we should call ourselves the Xyphoid Process Group."

I wouldn't have thought it possible, but somehow Plumpy had managed to come up with an even worse name than Gary did.

"Because, you know how everybody's got a xyphoid process," Plumps pointed just below his chest, "but it's kind of unusual at the same time."

I nodded and tried not to roll my eyes. "Um, okay. And Izmir, what do you have?"

Izmir stood, walked to the center of the clearing, beat his chest, and screamed. "The Ottoman Turkish Empire!" Then he walked confidently back to his log and sneered at me. "Just try to beat that, Peter."

The names were all so bad, this was going to be too easy. "Okay, those were all great, really great. But I think maybe we should go in a different direction. So listen, I was reading through The Book last night, trying to get some ideas, when I came across a section that was amazing."

"What was it about?" asked Plumpy.

I leaned forward and rubbed my hands together. "Meat." That perked them up. "Did you know that there was a time when the only thing men—*real* men—ever ate was meat?"

"You're kidding me," Gary said.

"I am not. Apparently, men would find meat, dry it out, and cook it, and then just keep hunks of meat with them at all times. And anytime they would want to eat it, they'd just pull these hunks out of their pockets and eat it wherever they were."

"Like celery?" Gary asked.

"Yep, just like celery. But actually tasty, because it's meat."

"What do they call this stuff?" Plumpy asked.

"That's the best part. They call it…"

I hesitated, and the guys leaned in closer.

"Beef jerky," I said.

"Say that again?" said Gary.

"Beef jerky."

"You didn't just insult my mother, did you Peter?"

"No way, Izmir, I learned my lesson the last time. That's really what they call it. But what's even better is, The Book gives detailed instructions for how to make beef jerky. And guys, that's what we're going to do. Right here in the woods. We are gonna *make beef jerky*. Four guys, learning to be men, *real* men, and making beef jerky, a real man's food."

"Wow. You really think we can do it?" asked Plumpy.

"I know we can. But listen up, because this is the best part. Do you know what we're gonna call ourselves?"

"The Four Boys In The Woods Group?" Gary asked.

"Sorry, Gary, I think I found something even better than that. We are gonna call ourselves... *The Beef Jerky Gang*."

I let that sink in, but by looking at their faces I could already tell how they felt.

We had found our name.

CHAPTER NINETEEN

A BEAUTIFUL NOTE

If we were going to make our own jerky, we were going to need a steady supply of our own meat. So, as our first official order of business, the Beef Jerky Gang decided we needed to figure out where the cafeteria was getting the meat it used for our mystery bits. Gary volunteered to sneak around and see what he could learn.

I was just settling into Mrs. Dorney's class on Monday morning, wondering if Gary had learned anything yet, when someone punched me square in the middle of my back and then slammed something on my desk. A familiar scent caught my nose—an aroma of peach with a hint of evil—as the Pink Dragon walked past me toward her desk.

My heart raced.

A note. On my desk. From Jessica Hale. The internal alarm in my head sounded. I had been preparing for this moment for weeks.

Over the years, I had received my share of notes from Jessica, and they were never good. But the Book had a special section on how to deal with notes from girls. Everything from how to actually unfold one, to how to read their loopy handwriting, to how to decode all those smiley faces and hearts.

Oh, and one more thing. How to use a girl's note against her.

I had started a few weeks ago, when I'd baited Jessica into writing me a nasty note. What she didn't know was that I kept that note—to use as a handwriting guide. It took me several nights of slow, painstaking work, but I finally mastered Jessica's ridiculous bubbly letters. I even learned how to make those obnoxious hearts that she put above her lowercase i's. I learned how to write like the enemy. And for the last two weeks, I had been carrying my *Jessica Hale Note Preparedness Kit* in my backpack at all times, just waiting for my opportunity to arise.

And now it had.

As I picked up Jessica's real note, I slipped my fake note out of my *Jessica Hale Note Preparedness Kit* at the same time. I unfolded both notes simultaneously.

Jessica's real note had only three words. The three words every boy dreamed of hearing:

YOU WILL DIE

Simple and to the point. You had to admire that about her.

Making sure no one was looking, I quickly slipped the real note in my pocket and pretended to read the fake note instead.

Jessica turned around and gave me a hateful look. So, she was on to me. Time to do something she would never expect.

I smiled at her and waved. "Thanks so much, Jessica!" I said it loud and proud.

My disruption caught Mrs. Dorney's attention immediately. She was a stickler about notes, and she shook her head at me. "Peter Mills, you know that notes are not allowed in this school. Who passed it to you?"

I gave the most innocent look I could muster. "But Mrs. Dorney, it was only Jessica Hale. No harm there, right?"

Dorney looked down at Jessica.

"Did you pass Peter a note?"

Jessica said nothing. She just sat there, simmering. Like her hatred for me was beginning to bubble out of her pores. This was fun. But it was about to get even better.

Mrs. Dorney walked to my desk, her hand outstretched.

"The note, Peter."

I shook my head. "That's not fair, Mrs. Dorney. It's a private note from Jessica to me, and I'd rather keep it that way."

"Well that's too bad, Peter. Rules are rules. No passing notes in class. You know the consequences: if it's important enough to disrupt my class, then it's important enough to be shared with the class."

And Jessica was just arrogant enough not to care. So what if the teacher found out that Jessica wanted me dead? That would just give Jessica the opportunity to explain to the class about how I was really the one responsible for the whole locker mix-up. I was sure she suspected me, after all.

But when Mrs. Dorney read through the note, she raised her eyebrow at Jessica and then cleared her throat. Her face reddened, and she whispered out of the corner of her mouth, "I must say, Jessica, I'm more than a little surprised."

Jessica folded her arms in defiance.

"*Dear Peter.*" Miss Dorney cleared her throat again as she shot another glance toward Jessica. All of a sudden, Jessica whipped her head around and looked at me. And just like that, her look changed from arrogant to very, very worried.

"*Dear Peter, I think you're super-duper cute. I was wondering if you would like to go out with me? Can't wait to see you later today at synchro!*

With Hugs and Kisses,

Jessica"

The girls in class exploded into laughter as Jessica shot up from her chair and snatched the note out of Dorney's hands.

"This is *not* my note!" Jessica screamed.

Mrs. Dorney couldn't hide the shock on her face. "Well, I am most sorry that you're embarrassed, but I'm afraid this *is* your note. I saw you put it on Peter's desk, though I was going to let it slide—until your boyfriend made such a fuss over it. Besides, I've read enough of your papers to spot your beautiful handwriting."

I'd never seen Jessica so mad. I think it was the word "boyfriend" that sent her over the top. I could see her teeth grinding as she read over the note, and the class continued to roll with laughter the whole time.

Then Jessica screamed at the top of her lungs. "CAPITAL-I-CAPITAL-M-*POSSIBLE*! This is *not* my note!" She ran down the aisle straight toward me, but on the way she tripped over Ernie Pile's backpack and went flying through the air, landing with a thud on the tile floor.

The girls in class continued to laugh hysterically. The boys appeared to be in such shock they didn't know what to do. But at least Plumpy was awake for a change.

By this time, The Falcon had appeared at the front of the classroom, and together with Mrs. Dorney, the two ladies managed to grab Jessica and pick her up while she was still screaming and kicking. Jessica continued to flip out as The Falcon took her out of the room. It's like the Ice Princess had a total and complete meltdown, and it was the single greatest thing I'd ever witnessed in my life. The *Jessica Hale Note Preparedness Kit* had worked. And better than I could possibly have imagined.

Plumpy and I laughed all the way to the cafeteria. We couldn't wait to celebrate our victory over Jessica. We grabbed our salads and hustled over to our table.

But when we sat down, I could tell at once that Gary and Izmir were in no mood to celebrate. They didn't even have their salad trays in front of them.

"I don't know what's wrong with you guys," I said, "but I guarantee you, our news will cheer you up."

Izmir shook his head and gave me a cold, hard stare.

"Put your salad trays away," he said. "We've got some bad news."

"Can't we at least count first?" I said, starting to look for my meat bits.

Izmir slammed my hand with his, making an enormous noise. But he didn't seem to care.

"Move away from the salad," he growled. "Gary has something to tell you."

CHAPTER TWENTY

THE BORING PARTS

"Good one, guys. I thought you just said the mystery meat is possum."

Gary looked like he was sick. Izmir stared at me like a part of him had died.

"Gary, don't mess with us."

Gary buried his face in his hands.

"But—but that's not possible," I said. "The mystery meat *can't* be possum."

Gary kept his face down.

"As in, the meat we eat every day in the cafeteria comes from *rodents*?" I said. "Animals that eat through our garbage at night, live in raw sewage, and eat pretty much anything they can get their claws on? In other words, generally the most disgusting creatures alive?"

"Well," Plumpy interrupted, one finger in the air, "technically, possums are marsupials, not rodents. You see, marsupials carry their young in pouches, and their teeth are quite different from a rodent's."

"Not the point, Plumpy."

He laughed. "I think it would be if you tried gnawing on a piece of wood without a pair of sharp incisors."

If I'd understood any of what Plumpy had said, I might have made some smart aleck remark. Instead I focused on our problem.

"And you're absolutely positive the meat we eat in the cafeteria is from possum?" I asked.

Gary nodded. "I was hiding in a garbage can outside the kitchen when the food delivery truck pulled up. A lady brought a cage of live possums to the back of the cafeteria and handed them to the cook."

I swallowed hard. *Live* possums? Only girls could find a way to make possum meat seem even more disgusting than it already was.

We sat there pondering our preposterous possum problem for the next few minutes. And the more I thought about it, the angrier I got. We lived in a world controlled by girls. A world in which they almost never fed us meat. Girls *knew* how much boys liked meat, yet when they finally gave us these few, *tiny* bits of meat in our lunch, it wasn't even real meat! It was the mangiest creature they could possibly find.

Possum.

And then it hit me. In all my years of school, I had never, and I mean *never*, seen a girl take any of the meat. I heard some deep breathing and looked up. Izmir was about to explode.

"They need to pray for this."

"Right thought, Izmir, wrong word. They need to *pay* for this, and you're absolutely right."

"They need to pay big time," agreed Plumpy while punching his hand with his fist.

"We could throw more stink bombs down the vents," offered Gary.

"Not big enough," said Plumpy.

"Plumpy's right. It's not big enough. Not even close. All this time they've been feeding us possum, and probably laughing like crazy because it's the only meat we get." I looked around the table at my three closest friends, fixing each one with a steely glare. "Drummond told me I needed to change things. Well, guess what: *right here*, and *right now*, the Beef Jerky Gang is gonna start changing things, *for real*. We're going to come up with the prank to end all pranks. It's time to show the girls of Finley they messed with the wrong boys."

We spent the rest of lunch brainstorming ideas. Afterward, as I headed to my afternoon classes, I slipped into the restroom to wash my hands. As I was drying them off, I heard a familiar creak, followed by the sound of the door closing. I looked up. It was Drummond, with his book cart. In the bathroom.

"Hi, Peter."

"Uh, hi, Mr. Drummond."

"Been looking for you, Peter."

I was getting tired of people looking for me in the bathroom. Drummond pulled a handkerchief out of his pocket and wiped his nose. Lovely.

"Peter, I told you to read the book, then come back down and find me so we could talk. Did you misunderstand me?"

"No, it's just I've been real busy."

He tapped his fingers together against the locked bathroom door. "I know. You and your friends *have* been busy."

I couldn't say Drummond looked happy. Nor did he smell real good.

"I don't remember saying that you could tell your friends," he added.

"Well," I shrugged, "not in so many words... But you *did* tell me to change things, and I needed their help."

"I told you to read the book and *then* change things."

"And I have." I didn't know what this was all about, but I really didn't have the time. "Sorry Mr. Drummond, can we do this another time? I gotta get to class."

Drummond slammed his fist into the hand dryer. "No, we can*not* do this another time." His nostrils flared, and little puffs of disgusting nose breath zoomed my way.

I was glad I'd already peed.

He pulled a tiny notebook from his front pocket and opened it up. "Let me see if I've got a good idea of what you and your friends have been up to. Let's see: first was the whoopee cushion in the cafeteria, then stink bombs in the hallways." His lower lip curled over his top lip. I was so confused. "You also flooded the girls' bathroom, put ketchup on the door handles, and sabotaged the principal's podium. Have I forgotten anything? Oh yes, of course.

The lockers." He closed the notebook and put it back in his pocket. "That's quite a list, Peter."

It really was. When all of the pranks were listed out like that, it was pretty darn impressive.

"How'd you know we did all those?"

"Remember, Peter, I *have* read the book."

"Good. Then maybe you could help me. The guys and I just figured out that all these years the mystery meat they've been serving us... well, there's really no easy way to tell you this, Mr. Drummond. They've been serving us possum meat."

Drummond's expression didn't change.

"Did you hear me? I said *possum meat.*"

"Yes, Peter, and about twenty years ago they used raccoons. When I was a boy, they used rats. Trust me, in the grand scheme of things, possum isn't too bad."

"You've *known*?"

"Yes."

"Then you know the Beef Jerky Gang has to make the girls pay for this! We need a prank to end all pranks. Can you help us think of something?"

Drummond shook his head back and forth.

"Just what exactly is the Beef Jerky Gang?"

"It's our name. We read about beef jerky in The Book, and once we find enough meat, we're going to make our own in the woods where we hang out."

Drummond didn't look so good.

"Peter, I need the book back."

"Don't worry, I've got it hidden. It's safe with me."

"That's just it. You've proven The Book *isn't* safe with you, and I don't want you to have it anymore." Drummond let out another stinky breath through his nose, his lips pressed together. "I was wrong about you."

My heart sank.

"I—I don't understand. Why are you doing this?"

"Peter, have you even read the book like I asked?"

"Every night."

"Really? Okay then, here's a quiz. An old lady is at a street light with a bag of groceries. You come up to her. No one else is around. Just you and her. What do you do?"

Long story was, I had no idea. Like I said, I'd skimmed over most of the boring parts, and an old lady with groceries definitely sounded boring to me. But I could make an educated guess.

"I'd push her over and take her groceries?"

Drummond rubbed his forehead with his hand, then shook his head and began to unlock the bathroom door.

"Fine," I said. "Maybe that's not the right answer. I didn't read that part, but who cares? We're doing the important stuff."

Drummond spun around. "No, what you're doing is playing a bunch of pranks to settle some personal scores. There's more to being a man than playing stupid pranks! And think about, just *think* about what happens when you guys get caught! You'll be done. And another opportunity to *really change things* will have passed."

He was right. I had never thought about it like that. Now *I* didn't feel so good.

"Okay," I said meekly, "the truth is... I haven't read the whole book. Some of it looked boring, and I kind of... skipped it."

"You don't say."

"But I'm willing to read it all. Please?"

He stared at the ground for a long while before looking back up.

"Can you give me another chance?"

"The girls would never give you another chance."

"I was hoping you might be different."

He nodded. "All right then. One more chance. Go home, read about the old lady, teach your friends, then repeat."

"The boring parts?"

"Yes, Peter, the boring parts."

CHAPTER TWENTY-ONE

AN APOLOGY

That night I started to read the other parts of The Book. They weren't cool in the same way that shooting a potato out of a piece of plastic tubing using a lighter and some hairspray is cool (page 132 of The Book), but they weren't boring like I thought they would be. Weird maybe, but definitely not boring.

The next day, I hustled into school early, excited to tell the guys, when I ran into something. Actually, some*one*.

Jessica.

I had been so consumed with thinking about possum meat and what Drummond said to me that I'd forgotten all about her. But of course, there was no way the Pink Dragon was going to let me get away with humiliating her the way I did with that fake note.

And unfortunately we were alone. Would she dismember me with her bare hands? Or would she do something more creative? I looked up to the ceiling. Maybe she planned to have a piano dropped on my head.

"I need to talk to you, Peter."

I looked her over carefully, trying to see what kind of weapons she might be hiding. Nervous that this might be my last conversation, I figured it was best to come out swinging. Verbally, at least.

"To finally talk about the crush you've had on me for so long?"

Her eyes narrowed into a squint but then quickly relaxed.

"The truth is, Peter, I was so mad when you did that stuff to me."

Okay… I figured I would play along. "What stuff?"

She half smiled at me, folded her arms, and rocked up and down on her toes.

"The fart noise in the cafeteria? I don't know how you did that. I don't know how you did any of those pranks. And making it look like I had something to do with it? Smart. Then last week, the lockers, and now that humiliating note in class?"

"I don't know what you're talking about."

"Whatever," she said with a roll of her eyes, "but I don't care, it's not important. Fact is, *someone* embarrassed me, and my first thought was that I wanted to kill you."

"And your second thought?"

"Still wanted to kill you."

"Third?"

She nodded. "But then last night I called my aunt—she and I are really close—and we talked for a long time. It took a while, but she told me that the way I felt is probably the way I've made *you* feel for a long time."

Huh?

"And now that I know how it feels... well, I just wanted to say..."

What exactly was going on here?

Jessica took a deep breath. "I wanted to say that I... I'm sorry."

Two cars collided in my brain. I found myself blinking to keep pace with my heart.

"I said I'm sorry, okay?"

Seriously, my brain was about to rupture from psychic trauma. Why was Jessica Hale telling me she was sorry?

And all of a sudden, something happened. I don't know how it happened, but it did: the usual dark cloud surrounding my mortal enemy was gone. All that was left was her perfect smile, long brown hair, sky blue eyes, and a bit of a peach scent—without the usual hint of evil. I was no longer looking at an ice princess or a pink dragon. Just a really cute girl standing in front of me, fidgeting with her hands and tapping her feet in figure eights on the tile floor.

She stuck out her hand.

"I really am sorry, Peter. For everything. And I hope we can get past this. Maybe start fresh?"

This had to be a trick. I looked up again for the piano. No hidden weapons. No fake exploding head. Just her royal cuteness and me. In a hallway. All alone.

I swallowed hard. A droplet of something wet rolled onto my belly from inside my shirt. Armpit sweat. Uh-oh.

I sent a message from my brain to my arm, and somehow, it responded. I watched as my hand moved through the air on its way into enemy territory. With only a few inches separating our fingers, Jessica locked eyes with me, then grabbed my hand and squeezed.

More armpit drops hit my belly. My throat got all sticky and full. The hairs on my forearm stood up.

Then Jessica pulled herself in close and whispered in my ear.

"That note wasn't all wrong, Peter. I do think you're cute. Maybe we could, you know, hang out sometime?"

A tingling sensation traveled from my neck all the way down the middle of my back until my legs started to falter. The only reason I didn't crumple to the ground right then and there was that Jessica was holding me up.

After lingering for what seemed like forever, she finally released my hand, backed up a few steps, giggled, then turned and walked away. Halfway down the hall, she spun back around and gave me a little wave.

I was in trouble.

CHAPTER TWENTY-TWO

A GENTLEMAN

Jessica smiled my way a few times that day. At synchro, she didn't yell at me once. And by the time the guys and I reached the woods, I was a complete wreck.

"So what were you all excited about?" asked Plumpy.

I looked up. The guys were staring at me, waiting.

"Excited about?" I asked, confused.

"You had something to tell us."

I needed to tell them about Jessica.

"Man, Peter, you don't look so good," said Gary.

But I couldn't tell them about Jessica.

"Did you find out where we can get some meat?" asked Izmir, tossing a pinecone into the trees.

It's like, in one day, she had changed.

"Or did you figure out what our big prank is going to be?" asked Plumpy as he stripped the bark off of a stick using a butter knife he had sharpened against a rock.

The guys would *not* understand.

"Earth to Peter... what is it?" Plumpy asked, snapping his fingers inches from my face.

I needed to forget about Jessica. Pretend it didn't happen.

"Er—I ran into Drummond... in the bathroom?"

"And?" Gary asked.

"He was mad about all the pranks."

That got their attention. All three of them leaned forward.

"He knew *we* did those pranks?" asked Gary, that old shiver starting again.

I nodded. "And he wasn't happy. He said I hadn't been reading the whole book. That there's more to being a man than pranks."

"So, what'd you do?" asked Izmir.

"Last night I began reading the parts I was skipping before."

"And?" Plumpy asked.

"Interesting stuff—but kind of weird, too. Any of you heard about being a gentleman before?"

Gary and Izmir exchanged looks and both shrugged. Plumpy looked uncharacteristically stumped.

"Never heard of it," said Izmir. "Is a gentleman what you become when you pull the biggest prank of all time?"

As angry as we all were about the possum meat, this gentleman concept was going to be difficult for the guys. I needed to take it slow.

"Not exactly. How about this: let me ask you guys some questions about gentlemen, and see if you can get them right."

They agreed.

"Question number one. Let's say you meet an old lady waiting at a crosswalk, and she's carrying a bag of groceries. It's just you and her, nobody else. What would a gentleman do?"

The guys huddled and discussed it. Plumpy popped his head up.

"Izmir wants to know if the gentleman is from the Ottoman Turkish Empire."

"I don't think that matters."

They huddled back together, and this time Gary popped his head out.

"Izmir says it does matter."

"Fine, whatever. The gentleman can be from wherever you like."

They broke up their huddle and Plumpy turned toward me.

"Okay then, Izmir and I agree that a gentleman would knock the old lady over and take her groceries."

Just how I had answered.

"And Gary?"

"I would get the old lady talking about something, maybe giving me directions. Then, when she wasn't looking, I would steal the salad out of her bag and replace it with my beef jerky. Can you imagine how mad she'd be when she found out she just had a bunch of strips of meat instead of her salad?"

I could tell Gary was proud of his answer, but he'd forgotten something of critical importance.

"But then you wouldn't have the jerky anymore. You'd be stuck with a bunch of salad."

His face fell.

"So who had the right answer?" Plumpy asked.

"I've got another question first. You're at a restaurant, and your buddy lets out an enormous burp. What would a gentleman do?"

Again the guys huddled together, but not for very long. When they turned back to me, Izmir had a big smile on his face. "We all agree this time. The gentleman would ask his friend how he created such an enormous and fantastic burp so the gentleman could one day learn to do it himself."

It was like I thought: the guys were really going to struggle with this gentleman thing.

"Guys, one last question, and I'll admit it's a tough one. You're walking alongside a girl down a street, and you notice a puddle of water coming up that's going to be hard to cross. What would the gentleman do?"

They huddled one last time. This time Plumpy and Izmir argued a bit before they turned around to answer.

"This was the easiest of the bunch," said Plumpy. "The gentleman would push her into the puddle."

"You agree, Gary?"

"Yeah, definitely push her in."

"Izmir?"

"I see the situation differently. If that gentleman was me, I would push her in, *but*—" He waved his hands excitedly. "Then I would make her friends watch so they could laugh at her. And then I would hire a hot air balloon to hover over her friends, except the hot air balloon is really filled with water not hot air, and then I would send a trained woodpecker to come by and poke a hole in the hot water balloon, and I would watch as all the water falls on her friends. And I would stand back and laugh at them all."

Izmir gave me a satisfied look, then sat down. What could I possibly say to that?

"Okay, so how surprised would you be to learn that none of you got any of the answers right."

"What do you mean, nobody?" asked Plumpy.

"Nobody. Not one. Not even close."

The guys exchanged confused looks.

"Question one: a real gentleman would actually try to *help* the old lady across the street. Question two: after your buddy lets out a huge belch at a restaurant, the gentleman is supposed to remind his friend to do that kind of thing outside. And finally, and this one is really tricky, when approaching a puddle with a girl, the gentleman would take his coat off and lay it across the puddle, so that she can walk across safely without getting herself wet."

The guys sat there in silence. Finally, Plumpy started laughing.

"That's hilarious! How'd you think of all that stuff?"

I sighed and shook my head. "No joke, Plumpy, it's all in the book. Those parts I skipped. A lot of them deal with being a gentleman."

"Well, if that's what a gentleman does, then I never want to be a gentleman," said Izmir, high-fiving Gary.

"Me neither," said Plumpy, breaking a stick.

"But guys, that's what Drummond was mad about. He told me pranks aren't enough. There's more to being a real man."

"Like this 'gentleman' stuff?" asked Plumpy.

"Exactly."

"Don't worry about it," said Plumpy, waving his hand in the air as if he were erasing those parts of The Book. "Drummond's a weirdo anyways. He hasn't been living in the real world for a long time. But we have, and that gentleman stuff sounds like a bunch of garbage."

"But we have to do it," I said.

"Do what?" Izmir asked.

"The gentleman stuff. Otherwise Drummond will take the book back."

"No way," said Izmir, crossing his arms. "No way we're giving the book back."

Plumpy raised his finger. "Izmir's right, and Bad Breath Drummond's a fool. You're telling me that after everything the girls have done to us and made us do, after all the crud they've put us through, after making us eat *possum meat*, we're just supposed to be *nice* to them? That sounds like the definition of insanity to me."

"Then what do I do?"

"Simple," Plumpy said while standing up and patting me on the shoulder. "You keep the book hidden and stay away from Drummond."

CHAPTER TWENTY-THREE

THE ENEMY HAS LANDED

Hiding from an old guy who spent his days in a dungeon was easy. Hiding from Jessica? Impossible. She waved to me in the hallway the next morning, talked to me before the start of Great Books class, and then while the guys and I sat down for lunch, I heard her voice.

"Hey, Peter."

The enemy had landed.

I spun around.

"Jessica?"

"Yeah, so Peter, I was wondering if... you wanted to eat lunch with me today?"

My throat started to close up and my face grew warm. I spun around and glanced at the guys, looks of terror spreading across their faces.

Izmir spoke through clenched teeth. "Pink Dragon alert, Pink Dragon alert."

Little late for that.

"Uh, I eat lunch here with my friends."

She looked at the guys, then at the rest of our broken-down table.

"There's room next to little Larry. I could sit there."

"It's Gary," a voice squeaked, as Gary slipped under the table and disappeared.

"Um, no thank you," I said.

She scrunched up her lips and nodded her head.

"Maybe some other time?" she said softly.

I tried not to do anything. I tried to sit still, to let this nightmare pass by. But as she stood above me, overwhelming me with her cuteness, I heard the sound escape from my mouth:

"Okay."

She giggled, gave me a little wave, then walked to her table. I turned and stuffed a handful of lettuce in my mouth.

"Peter, what the heck was that?"

They wanted an explanation, and I couldn't give them one. "She's been acting totally weird the last couple of days. I think she's got some prank she's trying to play on us."

I waited, hoping that just might satisfy the guys. Finally, Plumpy smiled and put his finger in the air. "Well of course the Pink Dragon won't go down easily. That's it: she's trying to soften us up, look for our weakness."

"Good thing that won't work," Izmir said, staring right at me.

"Yeah," I laughed, "good thing."

CHAPTER TWENTY-FOUR

ONE PROUD MAMA

I wasn't feeling so good after synchro, so I slipped away from the guys as soon as I had changed, and started walking home on my own.

A peach smell hit my nose as a hand grabbed my shoulder.

Jessica.

"Wait up, Peter."

She smiled at me, then twirled her hair around her finger.

"Hey Peter, have you thought about what I said, you know, about hanging out some time?"

It was all I had thought about. It was the reason I didn't feel good. But I thought I'd better try to play this a little more cool. Keep it simple.

"Flurrb." It was the only noise I could get to come out of my throat.

"What?"

Brain must try again. "Gloob."

"Peter, I'm not following you."

Stupid words couldn't get through my stupid throat. Best to stick to gestures.

I nodded.

She leaned in, her arms wrapped around her books. "So that's a yes?"

"Sure," I finally managed to say, my voice cracking in the process.

"Great! Hey listen, how about after our big synchro meet this Saturday, we could go out to celebrate afterwards."

Yikes, this wasn't a drill. This was for real. I managed another nod.

"Perfect, that new movie *Harriet Rides A Fierce Pony* is playing at the theater. We could go together, like a date."

I froze. I didn't know what to do or say. I feared that if I nodded, my entire body would fall over. All my extremities went numb—and I didn't even know what extremities were. Jessica must have shot me with some kind of invisible tranquilizer dart because right at that moment, I was paralyzed.

She saw that I was struggling.

"Oh, if you're worried about rides, my parents will do all the driving, and you'll be home by nine o'clock, I swear." She gave me a curious smile. "Will that work?"

I still couldn't get my lips to move and form words. I concentrated all of my brainpower on my neck muscles. Told them to move.

And I nodded my head one more time.

Jessica bounced on her tiptoes. "Great! I'm so excited and I can't wait." She spun and jogged away, and I was left behind, a pile of goo.

And then I came back to reality.

What had just happened?

I'll tell you what happened: I agreed to go on a date with Jessica Hale.

I walked home in a daze, ran up to my room, locked my door, and for the first time in a long time, I didn't even bother looking at The Book. Instead, I crawled into bed, stunned. Before I knew it, I had fallen asleep.

I awoke to a pounding on the door, followed by my mom's voice. "Peter, dinner time! I've got something to talk to you about."

I stumbled down the stairs, bleary-eyed. What could Mom possibly want to talk to me about? Whatever it was, it couldn't be good. It was never good.

Dad had cooked something that was green and orange, and that's about as well as I could describe it. Oh, and slimy—it was really slimy without taste. Dad was an expert at the no taste thing.

"So Peter, I guess you're wondering why I wanted to talk with you." My mother shoved a big forkful of the green and orange stuff into her mouth and chewed, little bits of orange squeezing out from the corners of her mouth.

By then I had woken up, and started to wonder what she could be talking about. And then I panicked. Had Mom somehow found out about the Beef Jerky Gang? Was an already terrible day about to become historically bad?

And then she broke into a smile and started to laugh.

"Why didn't you tell us you had a date?"

My dad and I both dropped our forks at the same time. I started to choke on the slimy stuff, so I grabbed for the spring water and chugged it.

"Excuse me?"

"You heard me. How could you keep something as exciting as your first date from us?"

How on earth could she know about this?

"Oh, I'm not mad, Peter. I know it's hard. Harold, that's why our Peter's been in his room so much lately. Moody, weird, this explains all of it… our boy is in love."

I'm sure my face went beet red. I know it got really hot, and sweat started to pour down my forehead, dripping into the slimy stuff.

"What are you talking about?" I said.

"Well, there I was, preparing to go home for the day, when our company's president, Margo Hale, popped into my office to say she just received a call from her daughter, Jessica, who was very excited for her date this Saturday with my Peter.

"I, of course, was astonished, but I've been around long enough to play it cool with the CEO. So I said that I'm sure Peter is excited too, but you know boys, he hadn't mentioned it to me just yet.

"Well how about that, Harold? Our Peter, going out with the most popular girl in school, Jessica Hale. Who would've believed that?"

My dad looked at me, then back at Mom.

"Yes, who would have believed it..." Dad stared at me a moment. Kind of like he was hoping I could pass him some secret information through my blinks.

"I'm sorry Mom, it just kind of happened real fast. It's not really a big deal—we're seeing a movie after our synchronized swimming meet this Saturday. Again, not a big deal."

"To the contrary, Peter, you dating the daughter of my CEO is in fact a very big deal. If things go well between you and Jessica, then things will probably go better for me at work. You know that promotion I've been gunning for? It's finally within my grasp. And with you dating Jessica, it's only bound to help."

"I think that's a little unfair to put that upon Peter," said my dad. "What if the date doesn't go well? Or what if Peter doesn't want to keep going out with her?"

My mom gave my dad that little sharp look she always gave him when he had just said something stupid or wrong.

"Nonsense, Harold. Peter knows how lucky he is to have a girl like Jessica Hale actually like him. He wouldn't screw that up. Plus, he's a smart boy, aren't you Peter? You wouldn't mess things up for your mother at work, would you?"

I looked at my dad, then back to my mom.

Yep, I was in serious trouble.

CHAPTER TWENTY-FIVE

SABOTAGE

I was in a no-win situation. If I went out with Jessica, I'd probably lose my friends; and if I *didn't* go out with Jessica, my mother would crush me.

Why had I agreed to go out with her in the first place?

I knew why.

Because she was pretty, good at everything, and because it really did seem like she had changed. But mostly, because she said she wanted to hang out with me.

The only solution was to tell the guys the whole truth. They would totally freak out about the date, but I would apologize and explain that I had gone temporarily insane. Then I would explain the jam I was in with my mother, and they would understand. These were my best friends. Together, we were the Beef Jerky Gang. They would *totally* understand.

I wanted to wait until lunch, so I mostly avoided the guys until then. And as had become normal by now, Jessica would smile and wink and giggle at me whenever she saw me, but I was able to get through the morning and was relieved when lunch finally came.

I grabbed my rice cake salad and noticed the guys were already together at our table. I weaved through the lunchroom tables and finally made it to the table and set down my lunch. "Hey guys, I wanted to talk to you about what happened yesterday."

I sat down in my chair.

The chair exploded, collapsing under my weight. I landed on my can and the only thing I heard was the cafeteria laughing.

At me.

I looked up and saw Gary, Izmir, and Plumpy staring at me. Each of them had a little hatred in their eyes.

"Traitor," Plumpy growled through his teeth. Gary and Izmir just shook their heads at me, then all three of them took their trays and walked to another part of the cafeteria. I could hear cries of "loser," "freak," and "dork" echoing throughout the cafeteria, and I noticed that even The Falcon was laughing at me.

The guys did this to me. They had sabotaged my chair. And that word that Plumpy had used: *traitor*. They must have heard about my date with Jessica before I could tell them myself.

I wouldn't be able to explain it to them after all.

And just like that, they hated me. So much that they decided to prank me in front of the whole school. I hung my head and walked out of the lunchroom. Alone.

CHAPTER TWENTY-SIX

THE NOODLES MEET

My best friends hated me and my mortal enemy liked me. According to The Book, if only my dog died and my truck crashed, I would really be in trouble.

I sat alone for lunch the next day. Jessica came over at the end of lunch period and told me it was embarrassing to have me sit alone when everybody knew the two of us were talking.

Talking? I'd never been talking with a girl before. Not ever. And the idea that I was doing it with Jessica Hale made me sweaty and nervous and—well, forget about it.

The entire situation with Jessica and the guys made me feel like I was walking around without enough oxygen. At least there was Saturday, our first synchronized swimming meet and then my date with Jessica.

There. I said it. My date with Jessica.

Having never been on a date before, I was terrified. And yes, she was my mortal enemy. But things had changed. She liked me. And I liked her too. I guess I had always sort of liked her. She was pretty. But it was more than that. She was smart. She was good at lots of things. What wasn't there to like?

Well, there was the fact that up until two weeks ago, she was a cruel, heartless, soul-sucking ice princess of a sixth grader. Sure, there was that.

But like I said, she had changed.

And I was more than a little proud to have had something to do with her change. The Book had given me the confidence to punch back, and once I did, the Ice Princess melted and all that was left was cute, nice, Jessica.

I could handle cute nice Jessica.

Saturday finally came, and the synchro meet was against our school's biggest rival, Noodles Junior High. We were all crammed into the tiny visitors' locker room at Noodles, watching The Falcon pace between us, looking uncharacteristically nervous. She wore a shirt that said "The Only Noodles I Eat Have Legs." Rumor was she'd dated the Noodles coach years before—until he stole her best synchro routine and used it against her in a meet. Finley synchro had gone winless against Noodles ever since.

"You may not know the sad history of our battles with Noodles, so let me speak simply. We *need* this victory today." She stopped pacing, then slammed her head into the nearest locker, looked up, and screamed. "KILL, MAIM, WOUND, DESTROY!"

I'll admit, I was a little freaked out. Even for The Falcon, this was fairly unstable behavior. But then she seemed to gather her wits, the crazy eyes went away, and she calmly scanned the locker room. "As extra motivation, if we don't beat those pedestrian pasta peddlers today, don't even bother picking yourselves out of that pool."

Maybe still not *entirely* stable.

As we followed The Falcon out of the locker room and onto the pool deck, boos rained down from the crowd, and we were treated to what was apparently a long and proud tradition at Noodles Junior High: pasta pelting. Spaghetti, mostaccioli, and bow tie noodles rained down on us like we were underneath an Italian rain cloud.

With so much starch flying through the air, it was hard to get my first look at the Noodle Press, one of the more famous and intimidating synchronized swimming venues in the region. The pool was circular, with bleachers all the way around it, like theater in the round. And this meant that as we walked in a circle around the pool, we were being pelted with hard shell macaroni from every conceivable direction.

The Falcon told us that pasta pelting was "nothing more than a minor irritant by a bunch of wuss-bag fans." Try telling that to poor Becky; she's the one who got a piece of linguini stuck in her ear. The Falcon had been unable to remove it, so she just jammed a piece of linguini in Becky's other ear to at least balance her out.

The dual meet had two components: team routines and the pairs competition. The Noodles team went first. They performed to Left Banana's "Fine China," a popular synchronized swimming song and one that lent itself to a more classical routine. And I had to hand it to them, they pretty well nailed it.

Then it was our turn. Jessica convinced The Falcon that it was time for Finley to announce our presence to the synchro world with a more cutting-edge and unorthodox routine, one with more room for error but also with greater opportunity for scoring. And for the unorthodox routine, we had chosen an equally unorthodox song: Nad Yennek's "Without Kittens." Both the routine and the song choice were risky, but The Falcon said that life without risk was like living without big biceps: possible but not really worth it.

We jumped into the water. I made sure my swim cap, nose plugs, and goggles were on tight. Jessica put her hand into the air and all of us followed. My heart was racing as we waited, and then the music began.

What happened next was mostly a blur. All the training, all the hard work… it was all for this moment. I'll admit, on that first day doing eggbeaters, I never thought I'd be able to do synchro. And yet here I was, part of a team—a team that was killing its routine.

When we finally finished, I totally expected another chorus of boos. Poor Becky was covering up her mouth and nostrils.

But nothing happened. The crowd was still and quiet.

And then a clap from the bleachers. Then another. And then the dam broke as the entire Noodle Press stood and gave us a standing ovation. The Noodles synchro fans might be tough and scary, but they also knew good synchro when they saw it—and we had just knocked their flip-flops off.

When the judges' scores went up, it was Noodles with an impressive 8.0 but Finley with a more-impressive 9.0, an incredible team score for a team that hadn't won anything in the last fifteen years. But we couldn't get too excited yet—because now was when things really got going. The pairs competition.

There were six pairs battles, and each was worth one point. Since we'd won the team portion of the competition by one point already, that meant Noodles would need to win four of the six groupings in order to take the meet.

Jessica decided to go first in order to set the tone. She and her partner Hillary destroyed the other pair and easily won. We were now up 10 to 8, and all we had to do was win two more pairings.

But Noodles wasn't going down easily. They won three out of the next four pairs, and as we headed into the final pair, the score stood tied at 11 to 11—just the way you'd expect a rivalry match to go. Which meant it was time for the final pair of the evening. A couple goons from Noodles against me and my partner: Plumpy.

Ever since things had gotten weird between us, I'd been concerned about being paired up with Plumpy. But as we both entered the water, I saw that Plumpy had an intense expression on his face. He evidently came to win. Just like me.

Jessica gave me a little wink from the pool deck and The Falcon pulled up her shirt sleeve a little bit so I could see her bicep Harry.

The whistle blew, the music started, and we were off. I felt strong in the water, the strongest I had ever felt, and I could tell that Plumpy and I were in sync today. Of course we were. Yeah, we were having a fight, but deep down, we were best friends for a reason—

and by about halfway through the routine, I had the distinct feeling we were kicking the other team's butt.

And then it happened.

The other team missed a turn. I could see it in my peripheral vision. It got them completely flustered, and they didn't regroup and get back in sync for at least ten seconds. They were finished—all we had to do was hold on. Plumpy and I were going to secure victory, our school's first synchro victory against Noodles in fifteen years. All we had to do was complete our routine. Just a few moves left. I looked over at Plumpy, and he looked back at me.

Then he smiled and mouthed a word.

Traitor.

And Plumpy started to sink.

He sank to the bottom of the pool, just like I'd done on our first day of synchro practice.

And as he sank, he also sank our chances at winning the meet. And he was sinking our friendship. The music ended.

A few adults jumped into the water and pulled Plumpy out. He, of course, gave an incredible sales job. He said he blacked out and couldn't remember anything. He asked if we had won the meet.

The voice over the loudspeaker gave the answer. Due to disqualification on Finley's last pair, Noodles had won the dual meet for a record sixteenth year in a row.

The Falcon went nuts. She went after the Noodles head coach but was blocked by the fans pouring out of the Noodle Press. So she did the next best thing: she threw a folding chair into the water. When one of the judges told her she would have to retrieve the chair, she threw the judge into the water. When that judge's husband told her to help the judge out of the water, The Falcon threw the husband into the water. Then she stormed out of the pool area, punching a hole through the door on her way out.

I sat on the pool deck, catching my breath, and watched as Plumpy, Gary, and Izmir walked back to the locker room.

Plumpy didn't do this to get back at girls or Jessica. He did this to get back at *me*. And I wondered, for the first time, if we would ever really be friends again.

CHAPTER TWENTY-SEVEN

FIRST DATE

I changed and met Jessica outside. She was breathing hard and her jaw was tight. Specks of blood covered her scraped-up knuckles.

"What happened?" I asked.

"I just finished what The Falcon started."

Great start to my first date.

Up ahead a large pink car pulled up alongside the curb and honked. A man in a dark suit and hat climbed out of the driver's side and hustled around to open up the back doors for us.

She whispered through gritted teeth, "That's our car."

I whispered back, "You have a chauffeur?"

She rolled her eyes, took a deep breath, and manufactured a half-smile. "It's my dad."

We climbed into the back. There were two rows of bench seats facing each other, and on one of them sat an older woman.

A brown-gloved hand shot out at me. I shook it with mine; she just about crushed it.

"Margo Hale, President of the Whitfield Corporation. I heard my Jessica is escorting you out on the town tonight. Your mother works for my company."

She didn't really phrase any of it as questions. Just statements. But the questions were about to start.

The whole way to the movie theater, Mrs. Hale asked me about my daily diet, what school of yoga our family practiced, and about how my chi was doing. I didn't even know I *had* chi, but Mrs. Hale explained that it was some life force I shared with plants and animals and the cosmos. After that, I told her my chi was doing very well but was looking forward to Sunday, its only day off.

The Hale women looked at me like I was a completely different species, and I heard Mr. Hale up front delivering the muffled-cough-laugh I'd heard so many times from my own dad. That's when I remembered that most girls didn't have a sense of humor.

Mrs. Hale made a couple of comments about my mom and how good her career was going and how she hoped I treated Jessica very well and didn't embarrass the Hale name this evening.

We finally reached the theater and I never thought I would be so glad to be alone with Jessica Hale in all my life. As we stepped out of the car and walked up to the theater I had a chance to really look at her. And then I looked down at me. I really couldn't believe a guy like me was out with a girl like her.

The movie was, of course, not something I was looking forward to. A girl riding a pony, even if it was fierce, was not exactly my idea of fun. But by this point in my life I had read so many books that were just as bad, I'd gotten skilled at faking interest. The best part of the whole show was getting to share a tub of baby carrots with Jessica. We ordered the new ones that were broccoli flavored. Not my personal favorite, but Jessica seemed to like them, and every once in a while our hands would dip into the tub of carrots at the same time and touch. She would giggle, sweat drops would attack my body, and a lightning bolt would shoot down my spine.

After the movie, we took a walk through a nearby park. At one point, she stepped so close to me that her shoulder touched mine. Then she slowly slid her hand down my arm until her hand landed into my palm and her fingers grabbed mine. I must have blacked out after that, because next thing I knew, we were sitting on a park bench and she was looking at me. Like she was waiting for me to say or do something. I must have missed something important.

She fidgeted with her lips, pursing them together in different figurations. She stared into my eyes, batted her eyelashes at me, and smiled. I had no idea what I was supposed to do.

I tried remembering the "how a gentleman acts on a date" section of The Book. There wasn't a door to open for her, there was nothing to pay for since her parents had paid for our movie, and there was no puddle for me to lay my coat over. What on earth was she waiting for me to do?

Then she opened her mouth.

"Peter." She batted her eyelashes again. "Why won't you tell me what you and your friends do for fun? What do you do when you hang out?"

I don't know what I was expecting, but I guess I wasn't expecting that.

"Well, right now we're not even talking... We're in a bit of a fight."

She sighed. "Is the fight about me?"

I shrugged. "Maybe a little. I'm sure it will blow over at some point."

"But when you weren't fighting, what did you do for fun?" Her mouth hung half-open, just waiting there. For something.

I couldn't really understand why this was so interesting to her. And then it hit me. She was *nervous*. My brain zoomed back to the section on how to take a girl on a date and I remembered something I'd forgotten. The very last part of that section.

Kissing a Girl for the First Time.

Idiot. That's what Jessica was waiting for. And when I blew it, she just got nervous and started asking anything that came to her. Of course.

I tried to remember what The Book had said to do. I wanted to act like a gentlemen of course. I grabbed her hand with mine, leaned in a little closer, and started to open my mouth. And then I heard something I wasn't expecting.

"Ew, Peter, that's gross!"

I knew that if you were doing this correctly, the girl was not supposed to say that.

Then Jessica pointed to her teeth with her finger. "Right there, Peter, you've got a big hunk of carrot stuck in your teeth. Get it out of there quick before I gag."

I was mortified. I stuck my fingernail between my teeth and swiped up and down until an orange carrot hunk fell out.

The two of us settled into an awkward silence. Sweat poured through my shirt. I was such a moron.

"So, Peter... I hate to ask the question again, but when you and your buddies leave synchro, I know you go someplace to hang out. I see you leave together practically every day."

Why did she care so much about me and my friends?

"I don't know, we just hang out. It's not a very big deal, okay?"

She looked at me again, moved in real close, and grabbed both of my hands.

"Then if it's not a big deal, can I come hang out with you guys some time?"

"These days, I think I'd rather just hang out with you."

She seemed to consider my response, then leaned back away from me. She was thinking. She swung her hair so that it brushed up against her cheek.

"Of course I appreciate that, Peter. I like you too... I've told you so." Jessica sounded impatient. I know what female impatience sounds like; I've heard it all my life.

"But I guess, I just don't understand what's so important that you have to do it every single day with your friends. Why can't you tell me about it? Are you doing something wrong?"

It was dark, but I was certain my face had just turned red. I wasn't prepared for these questions.

I looked at my watch. 8:30 p.m. The Hales would be picking us up anytime now.

I stood and started to walk back toward the theater.

Jessica jogged to catch up with me.

"How about this, Peter? I like you, and you, of course, like me. And I agree, we should spend more time together. So how about this? After practice on Monday, I'll meet you and the guys after synchro and we can all go hang out together. Okay?"

I didn't know what to say. I didn't know how to get out of this.

Mr. Hale was standing next to the pink car with the door opened. Mrs. Hale sat in the back, waiting for us to enter.

"Okay, Peter?" Jessica asked one more time, running her hands through her hair. "Can I please come hang out with you and your friends, please?"

Mrs. Hale snapped her fingers at us. I panicked.

"Okay, Jessica, I'll show you."

When the Hales dropped me off at my house, I had to endure thirty minutes of questions from my mom about the date. Finally, my dad was able to get her upstairs with the promise of a new organic antifungal cream he'd found—he said it would do wonders for the rough skin on her elbows.

As I lay in bed, all I could think of was the strange day I'd had. And just as I was finally about to fall asleep, I was startled by the music coming from my mother's "Me Room" down the hall. It was her favorite song, "I'm Special And I Know It." I knew what mother was thinking. Now that I was practically a member of Jessica's family, she was sure it would be no time before she was running the Whitfield Corporation for Mrs. Hale.

I had other concerns.

CHAPTER TWENTY-EIGHT

TRAITOR

After Monday's practice, Jessica met me outside the pool.

"Where's the rest of the guys?"

"They already took off. Hopefully they're still there, but like I said, we're in a bit of a fight."

She smiled and grabbed my arm, and we started walking.

"So, where are we going, Peter?"

"It's a surprise."

I figured this being-nosy thing was just part of being a girl. My mother had always kept pretty close tabs on where my dad was at all times, and this was probably similar.

But I wasn't about to take Jessica to the clearing.

I took the same streets I normally did when going home, and when I spotted the fabric store my dad frequented, I pointed it out to Jessica.

"I was a little embarrassed to tell you about it, actually, but there it is."

"Bernie's Fabric Store?"

I nodded.

"Yep, me and the guys are crazy about quilting. We regularly go into Bernie's, sometimes to buy, mostly just to look... and then we go to my house and quilt."

She narrowed her eyes at me. "You're kidding."

I sighed deeply.

"I wish I was. Like I said we keep it kind of secret, mostly because we don't want other members of synchro finding out and teasing us."

She looked puzzled. "But why would we? I mean quilting is so, so manly—so what's the big deal?"

"It might be manly, but it's the kind of thing dads and grandpas do. I didn't want you to think I was an old-timer."

She squeezed my arm and gave me a curious look.

"Show me."

"Really?"

"Mm-hmm."

The truth? My dad *was* a serious quilter, Bernie's was his favorite shop, and he had dragged me in there plenty of times throughout the years. So I knew Bernie fairly well and figured I could pull this off if I talked fast.

I pushed the door open and the bell rang. Bernie looked up from his morning paper.

"Hey, Peter!" he shouted.

"Hi, Bernie. Well, I'm back again, of course this time without my friends, unfortunately. We're in a bit of a fight right now—that's why we haven't been coming in to look at fabric as much. And our quilting output is way down."

Bernie looked at me cross-eyed. And then, like magic, something connected and his eyes lit up.

"No problem at all, Peter. I love it when you boys come in. Training the next generation of quilters—there's nothing quite like it." Bernie looked at Jessica. "But Peter, you're burying the lead. How do you come into the store with the prettiest girl in town without introducing her to me?"

Jessica shot out her hand.

"Jessica Hale, nice to meet you."

Bernie took her hand, and I could see him wince a little while he shook it.

"Not too often we get girls in here, Miss. What brings you by?"

Jessica looked around.

"Just wanted to see what Peter and his friends do all the time. You know, Peter tells me he comes by here after school most days."

Bernie just smiled.

"Is that true, Bernie?"

"Is what true, Miss?"

"Does Peter come in here after school most days?"

Bernie looked at me for a moment, and I squinted my eyes in response.

"Not every day, Miss."

"But most days?"

Bernie looked at me again.

"Yeah, most days… like I said, it's a joy to see him, he's a chip off the old block. His dad, Harold, well he's a bit of a quilting legend around these parts. Let me show you some of his stuff."

I could tell Jessica wanted to keep asking questions, but once Bernie got started showing off his collection of corduroy quilted pillows, there was no stopping him. A couple of times Jessica yawned, and at one point I think she fell asleep while standing, but finally, about twenty minutes later, Bernie took a breath and Jessica jolted upright.

"It was nice to meet you, Bernie." She was already halfway out the door. I turned and winked at Bernie, and he winked back.

Jessica was quiet as we walked away and I could tell she was deep in thought. We were near Skim Shady's, and though I came by here all the time, I'd never once bought one of their skims. I suggested to Jessica that we get a drink.

"You go first, Peter. I'm still trying to figure out what I want."

Simple was best for me.

"Okay, I'll get a double regular, with a twist."

The Skim Shady milk wench—his nametag read *Chuck*—poured me a large cup of skim. He squirted lime in it, then sprinkled parsley on the top for good measure.

Jessica stepped up. "I'll get a nibble skim, straight zero, cube of ice."

Chuck grabbed a jug marked "diet skim" and poured it into a tiny little cup. It looked just like water. On second glance, I was certain it *was* water.

Chuck grabbed a dash of powder, dropped it in the water, and mixed it up so the water turned a foggy white color. Finally he dropped a cube of ice into the tiny cup.

"And that's one zero nibble skim with a cube for the lady. Total comes to ten-fifty."

Remembering what The Book said about paying for stuff, I grabbed my wallet out of my back pocket. "Don't worry, I'll pay for it today."

Chuck the milk wench's mouth dropped open. I heard chairs scrape across the floor and before I knew it, everybody in the store was staring at us.

Jessica was hiding her face with one hand, and with her other, she was running her credit card through the swiper. She grabbed her nibble skim and took off.

"We're going now, Peter!"

We got half a block away from Skim Shady's when she unloaded on me. "I don't know what kind of stunt you were trying to pull back there, but that'd better not ever happen again."

"I—I don't understand. I was just trying to be nice. I thought offering to pay would be nice."

"It's not nice, it's *embarrassing*, that's what it is. You don't pay for my stuff. Don't you understand who my mother is? She's the president of one of the largest companies in the region, that's who."

She tore at her hair. "If my mother hears about this."

Jessica closed her eyes and took two deep breaths, then downed her five-dollar nibble skim in one shot. She licked her lips.

"Good?"

She nodded her head.

"But wasn't that just colored water?"

"It's a nibble skim, Peter. Totally different."

I wasn't so sure. I started sipping on my double regular with a twist. Pretty good, I thought. Maybe a little fancy for my taste, but good nonetheless.

We kept walking and were almost back at school.

"Peter, my mother's pretty influential at Finley. And anyways, she found out the region is sending a specialist to the school."

"Oh yeah?"

She folded her arms and stared at me. "It's an enforcement officer who specializes in what's called 'man practice.'"

"Sounds kind of interesting."

"It's not interesting, it's *revolting*. Anyways, I don't know if you've noticed, but things have been happening lately at our school. Unusual things."

"Like what?"

"Don't tell me you haven't noticed?"

I shook my head.

She leaned in toward me and looked around to see if anybody was listening. She was whispering.

"First that fart prank pulled on me—you know that day you made a fool of yourself falling in the lunchroom? Then the stink bomb? Then all sorts of pranks around school, including the one pulled on you the other day?"

I tried to give my best bewildered look.

"You know, the chair collapsing? The same thing happened to Ms. Higgins. It was sabotage. Anyways, this enforcement officer, I heard she's the best. She told my mom that all of this smells like boys mixed up in ancient man practices."

I could tell she wasn't making this up. Jessica's mother was powerful, and if she said this was happening, then it was happening.

"I just thought you should know and all." She looked down at her watch.

"Okay, I've got to go. I'll see you tomorrow."

Jessica strode off, and about a block away, a bubbly pink car pulled up to the curb and picked her up.

This couldn't be good. It didn't matter what was going on between me and the guys, this was too serious. Regional law enforcement didn't mess around. I had to warn the guys.

Fifteen minutes later, I was knocking on Plumpy's front door. Mr. Booms, Plumpy's father, answered.

"Hey, Peter." Mr. Booms stepped outside and looked around. "Where Leonard?"

"Oh, he's not with me. I actually came over to see him."

"That's weird. Leonard said he'd be hanging out with you."

I completely forgot: the guys were probably still at the clearing.

"Oh yeah, I couldn't today so that's why I came over. Anyways, could you just tell Plumpy that I'm going to call him tonight? It's really important."

"Sure, Peter, no problem."

I walked home and could smell the familiar fragrance of my dad's cooking as soon as I walked through the door. Dad's cooking may not have taste, but he did have a signature smell: *burnt*.

Of course, my mom could never understand how Dad had all that time at home to cook a meal and couldn't at least figure out how to cook it the right way. It was just another thing to clobber him about.

"Peter, is that you?"

"Yeah, Dad, I'll be up in my room."

"That's funny, you just missed your friends."

I stopped and walked to the kitchen.

"What are you talking about?"

"Your friends, Plumpy and Izmir. They were just here, said you and Gary were busy and you told them to come to the house and grab something." Dad pulled a steaming pot of goo from the oven. "What were you and Gary doing?"

"Wait a second, Dad. What did you give them?"

My dad shook his head while he stirred the pile of goo. "I didn't give them anything. They said you told them to go up to your room and grab it. Did they get it to you okay?"

Panic set in. I burst from the kitchen and ran up the stairs as fast as I could. I went in my bedroom and flipped over my mattress.

The Book was gone. In its place was a note with one word:

TRAITOR

CHAPTER TWENTY-NINE

SPECIAL AGENT TUNLEY

When I entered first period on Monday, Principal Lemming made an announcement telling us to head for the auditorium for an all-school assembly. Once the auditorium was full, Lemming rapped the gavel on her brand-new, prank-proof podium.

"Girls and boys, Finley Junior High is delighted to welcome a distinguished member of regional law enforcement to conduct an end-of-the-year review. Won't you all help me to welcome Special Agent Miranda Tunley."

A woman stood up to scattered applause, and for a moment I couldn't see her face because of the glare of the light. But then she stepped up to the microphone and came into focus.

Wow. She was a knockout. Like what an adult version of Jessica Hale might look like.

"Thank you, Principal Lemming, and thank you students. You darling students. What a beautiful school you have here at Finley. What an orderly school you have here at Finley. I will be spending the last two weeks of your school year getting to know all of you as part of a standard review of the school to ensure that it stays a beautiful and orderly school. I look forward to meeting and speaking with as many of you as I possibly can."

And that was it: end of assembly. Lemming dismissed us class by class, but I didn't hear a word she said. I was too busy staring at Special Agent Tunley. She was standing at the edge of the stage, carefully watching the students as they exited the rows.

Someone punched me in the shoulder.

"Eyes over here," said Jessica. "Come on, we've got to get back to class."

Special Agent Tunley might have been beautiful, but I could sense a danger beneath that beauty. With law enforcement at our school, I needed some advice. I needed to visit the dungeon.

I waited for third period, then slipped out with the "Need another diet book" excuse. As I walked down the hall, I saw Lemming, The Falcon, and Special Agent Tunley heading down a crossing corridor. I decided to do see what they were up to.

I heard them stop in the middle of the hall, so I inched quietly up to the corner and peeked around carefully. The three of them were bent down, inspecting one of the air conditioner vents we had used for our stink bomb. Special Agent Tunley was slipping on a pair of black leather gloves and nodded to Principal Lemming. "Timeline again, Lemming. Young Miss Hale has the fart explosion in the cafeteria, but no evidence is left because her father burned her skirt and the pink rubber attached, is that correct? Sounds like a classic whoopee cushion device." Tunley shook her head while Lemming and The Falcon exchanged perplexed looks.

Tunley unzipped her purse and took out a small tool, maybe a hair dryer. But as soon as she pressed its button, I knew what it was. A drill. And she used it to start unscrewing the metal grate. Over the noise of the drill she continued to speak.

"And then the school was evacuated by a strange smell. You had HVAC specialists, *male* specialists I'll note, come out and check out the scene and then you—" Tunley laughed out loud. "Then you canceled school for the rest of the day. Don't worry, darling: rookie mistake." She shook her head back and forth while The Falcon patted Principal Lemming on the shoulder.

Tunley yanked off the air vent, set it aside, and attached something to the tip of her drill. Then she pointed what was now a much longer drill up at the ceiling and squeezed the trigger. I heard something, like the sound of a small balloon getting popped, then watched as a projectile fired out and up and stuck into the ceiling. I could now see the projectile was a large dart with a black wire hanging down from it. A wire that Tunley pulled on and clipped to a belt around her waist. She gave the wire one last tug, then stuck a small flashlight in her mouth.

"Fortunately for me, men are pretty stupid. Makes my job easy. If there's evidence of criminal behavior, I'll find it."

And just like that, she jumped down into the air conditioning duct. The wire attached to the ceiling started to release, and I could see more and more wire coming out of the dart. I heard the unwinding of the wire as she rappelled down into the space, then a clang of metal as she hit the bottom.

"What are you going to do down there?" Principal Lemming asked, looking down into the dark hole at the base of the wall.

Footsteps echoed up through the air vent. Then a laugh. "Well, well, well. That didn't take long. What I'm doing, Lemming, is collecting the evidence that's lying right at my feet. Don't worry, I'll be back up in a flash."

And sure enough, thirty seconds later, the black wire started whizzing and winding back up, and Special Agent Tunley was back through the hole, on the hallway floor, unclipping the wire from her belt. She held a small plastic bag and wrote something on it with marker. She showed it to both Lemming and The Falcon.

"It's a broken eggshell. Old-school, crude device of course, but effective."

"What do you mean?"

"This, Principal Lemming, is a stink bomb. That smell in the school was no accident. And there was no air quality scare. This was premeditated. This was the work of boys."

Principal Lemming stepped back and covered her face with her hands. The Falcon pounded her fist into her hand.

"I'm sorry, Principal, but I don't need to find any more evidence. I've got all I need to classify this as a Section One Five Emergency."

"Which is?"

"Criminal Practice of Ancient Man Activity."

"For the love of McMasters, at *my* school?"

Special Agent Tunley put a hand on Lemming's shoulder. "I know it's hard, darling. Nobody ever wants to believe it could happen in their town, in their school—but it does. Don't worry, this is what I'm trained to do. We'll find whoever did this, and they'll be stopped."

"What do you need from me?"

"An office and a list of all your students. I've got a lot of work to do."

I ducked back behind the hall and dipped into the boys' bathroom. I heard the click-clack of high heels as the three women walked by. I held my breath and waited for them to pass.

This was worse than I could have ever imagined. This Special Agent Tunley was no joke, and as much as I needed to speak with Drummond, I couldn't with risk it with Tunley in the building. Nope, the best I could do was warn the guys.

When lunch came, I grabbed my tray and walked right over to them.

"I don't care what you say, I'm sitting down and we're gonna talk."

They slid their trays down the table and turned away from me.

"Guys, stop it, *now*. This is serious. This Special Agent Tunley, she's for real. I overheard—"

"Izmir, do you hear a small insignificant insect making a noise?"

"I think I do," Izmir replied.

"I know what that bug's called," said Plumpy, raising his finger in the air. "Traitortellus Annoyance Bugus."

"Plumpy, I don't care what you call me. We can figure all that stuff out later. What you need to know right now is that Tunley found one of the eggshells."

Gary turned and looked at me, his hand shaking. "How?"

"I saw her climb into the air duct."

"A girl climbed into the air duct?" asked Izmir.

I nodded.

Gary's lip quivered. "Well, if she'd do that, then she'd do…"

"Anything." It was Plumpy. "Okay Peter, we're listening."

But I didn't have time to say anything else, because right then Gary kicked me under the table and I saw Izmir's eyes get big. I turned around. Special Agent Miranda Tunley was heading straight for our table, clipboard in hand.

She smiled at us, took off her glasses, and chewed on the end of them for a moment.

"Hello boys, I'm special Agent Tunley." She pulled out a badge and waved it in front of us. "I'm with the Strategic Northern Offensive Taskforce. The S-N-O-T."

I saw Plumpy's nose wrinkle and I thought about what she said. And right as it hit me, I saw a big grin forming on Plumpy's face.

"You work for Snot?" Plumpy asked. Her smile was gone in an instant.

"No, not *Snot*, the S-N-O-T, the most highly trained enforcement officers in the region."

"But you still call yourselves Snot?" I asked.

I knew this lady was scary, but I just couldn't help myself. And it felt like, for a moment, things were almost normal with Plumpy and I.

"Listen boys, let's just say that I know how to break a man's femur in ten different ways."

I didn't know what a femur was, but it sounded bad.

"As you heard, I am conducting an investi—er, a standard review of the school, and I would like your cooperation. Names, please."

She spent the next five minutes asking us all sorts of questions about what had been going on lately at Finley.

And then she was gone.

I watched her walk away, then turned back to the guys. "Like I said, she's not messing around. You've got to lay low. Just please, whatever you do, don't pull any pranks until school's done and Special Agent Tunley goes back home, okay?"

Plumpy put his finger to his chin as if he was considering it. Then he shook his head.

"Hear this loud and clear. I'm glad the Snotty Special Agent is here. When you were a member of the Beef Jerky Gang, you were part of forming our mission. To eat meat and to get revenge on girls for ruining our lives. We still haven't made jerky, but after we found out about the possum, there's nothing that could stop me from getting back at these girls. And Gary and Izmir feel the same."

"But we *did* get them back, haven't we, guys? Think about all the pranks we've played."

"Not good enough. Not anything close. We've got something big planned. Something awesome. And frankly, I'd love to pull it off right under SNOT's nose."

"Plumpy, that's crazy, stupid, and it will never work.'"

"Peter, you're either with us or you're against us. And it seems pretty clear to us which choice you've made."

CHAPTER THIRTY

CALLING HER BLUFF

Three days later I was summoned to the temporary office of Special Agent Miranda Tunley. When I arrived, Tunley was sitting on the edge of a grey metal desk, legs crossed, reading glasses perched at the end of her nose, while she thumbed through a file with my name on it.

She looked up and smiled. "Ah yes, Peter darling, come in and sit."

Darling? I sat down on a hard metal chair and tried to scoot it back, but the chair wouldn't budge. I looked down and saw that it was bolted into the floor. A drip of forehead sweat fell. I heard the splash at my feet.

"Peter, I've been *so* looking forward to my talk with you, but I decided to make you my last visitor." She pulled lipstick out of her purse, applied a dark red shade, smacked her lips together, then stood and advanced toward me. "I think I have a pretty good picture of what's been going on around here, so I'll just need you to confirm some things. But first... take off your shoes and your belt."

"Excuse me?"

"Standard inspection, Peter. Every student has to do it. Shoes and belt."

I didn't feel comfortable about this.

"Now," she growled, stomping her high heels inches from my feet.

I removed my shoes while she kept talking.

"Peter, I catch bad guys for a living. And it is my professional observation that bad guys hide bad things in the craziest places."

She examined the shoes carefully and then the belt.

"Okay, next is your wallet."

I rolled my eyes, but she just folded her arms and stared down at me. I gave up my wallet, which she looked through slowly.

"Isn't this an invasion of my privacy or something?"

"That's funny, people only worry about privacy when everything seems normal. But trust me, if things get out of hand around here, privacy is the last thing you'll be worried about."

"So it *is* an invasion of my privacy?"

"Sure, but Peter, this whole school is a Section One Five Emergency."

"What does that mean?"

"It means that there is no such thing as privacy anymore."

I slumped back in the hard metal chair.

"Okay, wallet's clean. What else—eyeglasses?"

I shook my head.

"Retainer?"

"You're kidding, right?"

"Jewelry of any kind?"

I thought for a moment.

"All I've got is this chain." A chain that held a locket, actually. Inside the locket was my favorite picture of my dad and I from when I was little. Dad had such a big smile on his face, he looked almost alive.

She nodded.

I grabbed it from around my neck and handed it over.

"It's got a picture? For a special lady maybe?"

"Just a picture of my dad and I. Nothing really."

She took something from her purse, like a magnifying glass, and held it up to her eye. She examined the locket and chain closely.

"You wear this chain often?" she said without looking up.

"All the time. Listen, what's the problem?"

She looked up. "No problem at all, Peter, the locket looks clean. Put your shoes and belt back on."

I slipped my shoes on, tied them, and strung my belt back through my pants. Tunley handed me my chain.

"Can I go then?"

"Darling, we're just getting started. Now is the time for our little chat. I'm more of a visual learner, so I've got some pictures for you, okay?"

She took out a different file and pulled out some photos.

"Peter, these are pictures I took at the Correction's National Detention Center. Do you know what a detention center is?"

I shrugged.

"It's a prison. A prison is where bad guys go. A prison is where they take away all your freedom and somebody tells you when you can go to the bathroom and what time you can eat."

"So a prison is a lot like school?"

"Funny. I heard that about you: funny boy, always quick with a smart comment. I've met boys like you before. They were funny too. But let me tell you a little secret." She leaned in and whispered in my ear. "The funny ones always scream the loudest when I take them away. The prison guards tell me the funny ones cry for their daddies at night. You hear what I'm saying, Peter?"

"I really have no idea what you're talking about."

She grabbed the back of my neck with one hand and with the other she jammed a photo in my face and smeared it around against my nose. I coughed until she backed the picture up.

"See this boy, Peter?"

Tunley pointed to a young boy wearing a pink jumpsuit and standing with a bunch of older men who were also wearing pink jumpsuits. They were standing in a line, waiting to eat.

"I took this picture of my little friend Ralph the first day he stayed in prison. Can you guess what was particularly special about that day for Ralph?"

"No idea."

"It was Ralph's eighth birthday. Now here's the part that's really funny. I had the evidence to bust Ralph a few weeks before, but I waited—because I thought how fun it would be for little Ralphie to spend his first day in prison on his birthday."

This lady was out of her mind.

"Are you understanding me, Peter?"

I swallowed so hard I was sure she could hear it.

"I'll take that as a yes. So Peter, I think I've got the picture of what's been happening at Finley. A group of boys discover something that teaches them about ancient man customs. Curious, these boys start practicing these customs themselves, and before they know it, things have gotten out of hand. And you, of course, are right in the middle of it." She let that hang there while she danced her fingertips together. "Just like your friends told me."

What?

She studied me, trying to gauge my reaction.

No way. The guys were mad at me, that's for sure. But they would never, ever rat me out.

"Peter, I've got eyewitnesses that tell me you're mixed up in all this suspicious man activity. But if you come clean right now and tell me the truth, I'll make things easy on you."

She studied me again, and for some reason, my mind drifted back to The Book, to a section on playing a card game called poker. Apparently a big part of poker was learning how to "bluff": to make people believe you had something, when you really had nothing. And in an instant, I could tell that Special Agent Tunley was bluffing.

She had nothing. At least I hoped.

I smiled. "Special Agent Tunley, let me first say how happy I am that you're here to clean up this mess. I agree, these ancient man… costumes, did you call them?"

"Customs," she said.

"Right. These ancient man customs just can't be allowed, and you've got to find the culprits. The idea that I would have anything to do with boys like this is more than a little absurd. Right now, my life is about school, synchronized swimming, and my girlfriend, Jessica Hale."

I locked my hands behind my head, leaned back, and stretched out my legs. Time for *me* to study *her*.

Tunley narrowed her eyes a little then slid her pointy finger down from the tip of her nose until it danced along the corner of her chin. "You sure about this, Peter?"

"Yeah, I'm sure."

"Because that is not the story I'm getting from your friends."

I needed to trust my gut. This lady was bluffing.

"I can't believe that, Special Snot Agent Tunley, since it's not true. Neither my friends nor I would ever involve ourselves in something so dirty and despicable as *man* activity. But, in case somebody has lied to you and told you I *am* involved in this…" I looked around and motioned for her to come closer. She bent down, her face now just a few inches from mine. "I think I know why they might tell you such lies. Fact is, they're out of their minds."

Special Agent Tunley ran her hand through her hair. She chewed on the corner of her lip. "Really? Out of their minds?"

"Certifiably crazy. Miranda—may I call you Miranda?"

"No."

"You may not know this, but you're probably the most beautiful woman any of us boys have ever seen in our lives. And frankly, just being this close to you, I feel like I'm going a little crazy myself."

That ought to do the trick.

She stepped back a few steps and breathed through her nose, her lips pressed together.

"Last chance, Peter."

"If I thought you'd say yes, I would ask you out on a date right now."

"You will go down for this, Peter Mills."

"I assume if you really had proof then I'd already be in one of those pink jumpsuits. But since I'm just a law-abiding boy who is as repulsed by this man nonsense as you, I assume I'm free to leave?"

"Fine."

"Yep," I said. "Just fine." I jumped up and headed for the door, expecting her to throw something heavy and sharp at the back of my head. But it never came. As I jogged out of her office and down the hall, I found myself thinking that I had just dodged major trouble. And as scary as Special Agent Tunley was, I was frankly surprised she had fallen for my bluff. Maybe she wasn't as tough or as smart as she thought.

CHAPTER THIRTY-ONE

THE CLEARING

With two days of school left, Jessica caught up with me after synchro practice.

"Hey, stranger," I said.

"Yeah, about that… sorry, been busy. Lot of stress with end-of-year exams and getting ready for the big synchro meet."

"Yeah," I agreed, "my mom said she'd disown me if I didn't do well on finals this year."

"Harsh."

"She usually is."

"Listen Peter, we need to talk."

This didn't sound good.

"It's about us. Tell me the truth. Do you like me or not?"

I shrugged. "I went to the movie with you, didn't I?"

"But do you *like* me?"

"Yeah."

"How much?"

"How much?"

"Yes, Peter. How much do you like me?"

"What do you mean?"

"I asked what you and your friends do because... well... because I want to know the real you."

"I took you to Bernie's."

"Yeah, about that." She shook her head. "Sometimes I feel like maybe you don't like me as much as I like you."

"No, but I really do like you."

Her eyes relaxed. She stepped toward me, almost standing on my toes. We were face to face, almost nose to nose. I didn't know what was about to happen, but I knew I was entering uncharted territory. I felt a big drop of sweat fall from my armpit and roll down my belly. Apparently I still had a little squish left.

She took a deep breath, bounced on her tiptoes, and ran her hand through her hair. Then she bit her lip. "That sounds great, it really does—but words only mean so much to a girl. Actions speak louder than words."

"Actions?" My voice cracked.

She nodded, a dimple forming at the edge of her smile.

My mouth went dry. I tried to swallow, but something was ripping at the inside of my chest. I felt like I was choking. I looked at Jessica again. I *was* choking. I'd never felt like this in my life. Not ever. I wondered if my dad had ever felt like this. I pictured the way he looked at my mom: like a guy half-asleep, half-dead. Maybe, in some strange way, Jessica and I were meant to be together. Boy meets Girl. Girl humiliates Boy repeatedly. Boy hates Girl for most of his young life. Boy finds Book. One day, Boy starts acting like a real man. And everything changes.

Jessica stared at me, her long eyelashes blinking more than normal. That was it, of course. The moment I'd started acting like a real man, her pain-in-the-butt, perfect, mean-as-an-ice-princess shell started to crack, and all that was left behind was a big puddle of cuteness.

She was waiting on me, and this time there was no broccoli-flavored carrot chunk to stand in my way. I leaned forward, closed my eyes, and began to open my mouth when…

A cloud of finely misted snot exploded into my face with tremendous force. She had sneezed right in my face.

"Oh, Mother Peter, I am so, so sorry."

I'll admit, getting sneezed on at point-blank range wasn't exactly my plan.

She twirled around and snapped her fingers. "Actions, Peter. Good try with Bernie's Fabric Store, but I just can't believe you and your friends hang out quilting all the time because if that's what you really do, then I'm not sure I want to hang out with you. To be honest, quilting is kind of lame, and I—I just thought you were cooler than that."

She inched forward even more and whispered in my ear. "Peter, show me the real you, the kid that all those years, even though he drove me crazy, I secretly liked, I looked up to, the kid who had backbone, who wasn't afraid to put up a fight. Show me that kid."

A hot-and-cold mixture shot down my spine and out to my fingers, and the hair on my arms stood on end. I was excited and scared all at the same time. I needed to step up and be the man of action Jessica needed. Unfortunately, the point-blank sneeze had pretty well killed my preferred course of action. But there *was* something else.

I looked down at my watch. The guys might still be at the clearing.

"There *is* something I could show you, but not now, it's too dangerous. Think you could meet me after dinner?"

Her eyes danced. "Dangerous? I like the sound of that. You got it, Peter. Where?"

"Skim Shady's at seven. We'll walk from there."

Some kids might consider going out for a secret meeting with a girl to be a tough sell with the parents. Not me.

"Mom, would it be all right if I meet Jessica after dinner down at Skim Shady's?" We were all seated at the dinner table.

My mother put down her newspaper, a smile covering her face, then mussed up my hair.

"Like you even need to ask me such a question. Of course you can." She turned to Dad. "Harold, do you hear that?"

"No dear, what is it?"

"I hear my music."

"No you don't dear, that's the dishwasher."

Mom stood up and started swiveling her hips and moving her arms around like a beetle lying on its back. "No, Harold, I most *certainly* hear my music."

And before my dad or I could stop her, mother was singing "I'm Special And I Know It" right there at the dinner table. Dad plopped his forehead into his dinner and I left.

Jessica was right on time, waiting outside Skim Shady's. She looked incredible, like an angel sent from above. An angel that can dismember you with her bare hands and occasionally sneezes in your face from point-blank range.

"Where are we going?" she asked, a smile lighting up her face.

"You said you wanted to see the real me, right?"

She nodded.

"You said quilting was lame, right?"

She nodded again.

"Then come with me."

We walked through the alley next to Skim's. I looked around to be sure nobody was following. Then I took a look at the woods and grabbed her hand.

"What are we doing, Peter?"

"We're running."

I took off, pulling her with me, and together we into the woods as fast as we could. She pulled her hand away from me when we'd made it some ways into the trees.

"Peter, where are we going?"

"You said you wanted to see where the guys and I really hang out."

"But Peter, nobody's allowed in the woods."

"Do you want someone who follows the rules and quilts, or do you want someone less lame?"

She squinted her eyes at me. "Less lame."

I pulled a blindfold out of my pocket. "Then you've got to wear this."

She pulled back. "No way. Especially not at night, in a forest."

I shrugged. "Then you're not going to see where we hang out. It's as simple as that."

She turned around and took a step away from me, then wheeled back with her hands on her hips. "You let me fall and I'll kill you, Peter Mills."

I tied the blindfold snugly around her head, then began to lead her through the forest. I wasn't a total idiot. I may have liked Jessica, but I still didn't trust her, not completely. I took her through the woods slowly, twisting, making circles, crossing the creek, then crossing it again, and finally crossing the tree. Then I walked around the clearing, twisted a few times, took a big circle, and finally came back. We entered the clearing and I looked around.

"We're here," I said, taking off her blindfold.

She blinked several times, adjusting her eyes to her surroundings. The moon and stars were bright enough to give the clearing just enough light. She walked around, looked at the fallen trees, then opened her arms, palms up.

"I don't get it. There's nothing here. What do you guys do?"

"Mostly, we hang out. We talk about the kind of stuff we want to talk about. Spend time together, just being friends."

She folded her arms. "Don't tell me this is where you quilt."

I shook my head.

"So what do you do here?"

"What would you say if I told you 'not being lame' meant we had to break a few rules?"

"Peter, I'm not some rat fink goody two shoes, okay? I'm breaking rules just being here with you. Come on, what do you do?"

"We make jerky."

"You do what?"

"We make little strips of meat that we dry and cook and then keep around in case we ever want some meat. In case you've never noticed, we don't get much meat."

Whatever she might have been expecting, it wasn't that. I think I genuinely surprised her.

"You couldn't possibly make up something as stupid as that, so I'll assume you're not kidding."

"Nope."

"What else do you do? Is this where you learn to pull pranks?"

"No way."

She narrowed her eyes at me.

"Jessica, I'm telling you the truth: that's not us. We never did any of those pranks. I wish I knew who was doing them, I just know it's not us. We make beef jerky."

"But why?"

"Because we're hungry, and we like meat, and we barely ever get meat. If it's breaking a rule to eat when you're hungry, then yes, we're breaking a rule."

She walked around the clearing, picked up a couple of sticks, and threw them into the woods. "I gotta be honest, Peter, I wasn't expecting this."

"But is it cool?"

"I'm not sure 'cool' is the right word. It's weird, and you're taking a big risk coming into the woods, so I guess it's not lame."

Then she looked down at her watch.

"I better be getting home."

I held up the blindfold and she frowned.

"Sorry, whether or not you think it's cool, being in the woods *is* against the rules," I said. "And right now, with someone like Special Agent Tunley wandering around town, I'd like to avoid getting busted for anything."

"Tunley can be a little scary," Jessica said.

"But boy, is she pretty."

"Watch it, Peter." Jessica punched me in the shoulder.

I put the blindfold on her and walked her carefully back through the woods, making sure I took a different route than last time. Fifteen minutes later we came out behind Skim Shady's.

"Okay, Peter, I believe you."

"About what?"

"You really do like me."

And she turned and jogged away.

CHAPTER THIRTY-TWO

A BLINKY RED LIGHT

Showing the clearing to Jessica was a big step. Maybe not "rubbing anti-fungal cream on the bottom of her feet" big, but pretty close. And the next morning, I was so excited to see her again that my walk to school felt more like I was floating on a cloud.

And trust me, if I could find a less girly way to describe it I would.

I didn't even notice when a pink school bus edged up to the curb of the sidewalk and practically sideswiped me. Then I heard that familiar cackle and looked up to see Margie and pink bus number fifteen driving away. But on this particular morning, I had no hatred for that bad-makeup, bus-driving beast. Instead, I felt sorry for her. I was pretty sure she didn't have anybody with whom she could share a secret.

I, on the other hand, had found someone. And I was happy. My only real problem was being in danger of pulling a muscle from smiling so hard. I needed to see Jessica. To say hi. To watch that cute dimple form at the edge of her mouth.

I waited by her locker before school, watching the doors where she entered the building every day. I waited. But she never came. Morning bell rang, and the kids in the hall started racing around to their first-period classes. Still I waited, and still no Jessica.

Jessica Hale never missed school.

She didn't show up to first period. I spent the next two passing periods watching for her in the halls. I expected that at the very least I would see her in Mrs. Dorney's class.

But she wasn't there.

Jessica was missing, and I was worried. The only way she would miss school was if she was sick, and that would be a complete disaster for our synchro tournament the following day.

I'll admit, I may have hated synchro the first time I hit the pool. And yeah, okay, there were plenty of times I still hated synchro. But something about working hard and pushing myself and competing as a team... well, I wanted to see this through. I wanted to win. And in order to win, we needed Jessica. *I* needed her.

I had just about given up on seeing her at all when at last I found her that afternoon sitting at her desk in Ms. Higgins's class. Her head was in a book, and she was reading intensely.

"Jessica, thank goodness you're okay. Where have you been?"

She raised her chin, looking kind of annoyed. Then she shook her head and forced a smile.

"Sorry, Peter, bad day. I've got a ton of studying to do." Then she dropped her head and went back to reading.

My heart was about to explode and all she could give me was "bad day"?

She looked back up. "Seriously, Peter, not now. I have to study."

"But?"

She shook her head, pinched her fingers together, and ran them across her pursed lips. She zippered me.

I tried talking to her again at the beginning of synchro practice, but before I could catch her, she dove into the pool and started barking instructions at the team. Something was definitely wrong.

Or maybe not. This was our last day of practice before the big meet. Tomorrow was final exams. And Jessica *did* like to be perfect at everything. She was probably just stressed. That must be it.

At least that's what I told myself as I sat in the locker room after practice, packing my one-piece in my bag. As had become custom since we'd been fighting, the guys were changing in another row of lockers so they wouldn't have to hang out with me. I heard them laughing and joking with each other. I sure missed hanging with them. But I told myself that would all change this summer.

A sudden knock on the door startled me. It opened and Jessica poked her head around the corner. "Hey Peter, are the guys still here?"

"Sure, why?"

She banged her fist against the nearest metal locker. "Hey knuckleheads, gather round for a quick word with your captain!"

All at once, I heard Izmir say something in Turkish, Gary whimper, and Plumpy kick a locker. Then the three of them came around the corner.

"Good. Just a final reminder to you boys of how important tomorrow's regional meet is. I didn't agree to captain this team for my health. I did it to win. I want to make sure each one of you does everything in your power to make sure we bring home victory for Finley and for Coach Falcon. But most importantly, for *me*." She jabbed her thumb at her chest, as if we didn't understand the word "me."

Then she shook her head and laughed. And not the friendly Jessica laugh of late. This was pure Ice Princess. "I sure wouldn't want to be the one that screwed this up for the team." She scanned the room, but her eyes settled on Plumpy. She clearly hadn't forgotten the drowning episode that had lost us the Noodles meet.

Then she stepped toward Gary and slapped him on the shoulder. "Good luck tomorrow, Kerry."

"It's Gary." She ignored him.

"Izmir, we need your best tomorrow." Izmir didn't even try to remove the scowl from his face.

She moved onto Plumpy.

"Well, well, well." She cracked her knuckles. "Like I said, better not let anybody drown—er, down." Plumpy rolled his eyes.

And then she stepped over to me.

"Peter, you need to be at your absolute best tomorrow. A-plus. Nothing less. You got it?" Then she started to walk away.

Huh?

"Wait a second, Jessica, hold up."

She spun around, and that annoyed look was back on her face. She checked her watch, then tapped her foot against the floor.

"Make it fast, Peter. My aunt is taking me shopping."

I was so confused. She'd wanted to know the real me, and I'd showed her the clearing. When we were done, she'd seemed happy. So what happened?

"I—I just wanted to know if…" I heard sneakers squeak on the floor and suddenly I was conscious of the guys behind me. I leaned in and whispered. "If you had a good time?"

"Last night?" she said, a little too loud.

"Yeah," I whispered again.

She rolled her eyes. "Yes, I had a good time going to your little spot in the woods last night, but I've got a lot on my plate now, okay?" She glanced at her watch. "Like I said, I've got to go shopping with my aunt."

And then she spun around, pushed open the locker room door, and was gone.

I heard a shuffling of feet behind me as Jessica left the locker room, and I stood there frozen. Behind me, I could hear breathing. Deep, angry breathing.

I commanded my mushy brain to tell my limbs to move, and very slowly, I turned around.

Gary, Izmir, and Plumpy just stared at me. With wild, angry eyes.

Then, like he was shot out of a cannon, Plumpy launched himself right at me, screaming like a maniac. His shoulders hit me right in the stomach and he rammed me into the steel locker behind me, where the lock jammed into the small of my back. The two of us fell onto a bench and rolled onto the locker room floor. Plumpy pinned me and straddled me, swinging wildly at me with everything he had.

"How could you, Peter? You no-good, girl-loving, boot licker. How could you! How could you show her the woods? You traitor!"

It all happened so fast, all I could do was cover my face. Gary and Izmir finally pulled him off of me.

Plumpy had gotten plenty of good shots in, but at the moment I didn't care. I just lay on the cold locker room floor and stared up at the fluorescent lights flickering above me.

I finally sat up and looked at Plumpy. He was sitting on the bench now, shaking with anger.

"How could you, Peter? After what she's done?"

I just shook my head, a thousand things rushing into my head at once.

Izmir picked Plumpy up. "Let's get out of here."

"Yeah," said Gary. "We'll go back to your house and figure out what we're gonna do."

"Guys, I screwed up. But I'm not stupid. Yes, I took Jessica to the clearing last night. I admit it. But I blindfolded her, and I took her in a bunch of figure eights. There is no way, and I mean absolutely *no way*, she could ever find that clearing again. You guys are safe."

Plumpy stood there, seething. One hand on his hip, the other clenched in a fist. Gary crouched and picked something up.

"Peter, this is that picture of you and your dad that you keep in your locket, isn't it?"

He handed it to me, and sure enough he was right. The picture must have fallen out of the locket while Plumpy and I were fighting.

I felt around my neck. The locket was still there. I opened it up, grabbed the photo from Gary, and was about to put it back in the locket when Plumpy's eyes grew huge. He grabbed my locket and pulled it closer. We were practically nose to nose.

"Peter… tell me there's a really good reason you have a blinky red light in your locket."

"What?"

I snatched my locket away from him and looked.

A red light. Pulsing. *On. Off. On. Off.* Right where I usually kept the picture of me and my dad.

"I… I don't understand. I have never, and I mean never, seen this light before. What is it?"

Plumpy shook his head at me. "I know exactly what it is. I saw something like this in one of my mom's old electronics books. It's a tracking dot. Works on a radio transmission."

"A tracking dot? What are you talking about?"

"I'm talking about the fact that in addition to ditching your best friends for a girl, you also screwed up big time. You think you're so smart. Well, looks like somebody was smarter than you, because wherever you've been, somebody knows. Somebody's been *tracking* you."

Gary looked at me with hopeful eyes. "Peter, you never take that locket off. Who could have put a tracking dot in your locket?"

An image flashed of a pair of finely manicured hands giving me my locket back. I put my hands to my face and slumped forward. I ripped at my hair with my hands, spun around, and kicked the nearest locker.

"Peter…" Plumpy said through gritted teeth. "Who put the tracking dot in the locket?"

I didn't want to tell them. I didn't want to admit what I'd done, how stupid and reckless I had been.

"Peter?" Izmir said, his jaw tense, his eyes angry.

"It was Tunley," I spat out. "Special Agent Tunley. She made me take the locket off so she could check it out. I just thought she was hassling me, trying to scare me. I didn't think she could…" I looked up. All three boys looked back, like they didn't know me anymore.

I couldn't believe what I'd done.

Plumpy shook his head in disgust, then raised his fist in the air. I just stood there, waiting for the punch to come. Whatever he did to me at that moment, it wouldn't matter. Not after what I'd just done.

"He's not worth it," said Izmir as he stepped around me.

Plumpy's face twitched, and that vein in his neck was bulging.

"Not anymore."

He, too, stepped around me and left the locker room. They all did. I stared at the door, trying to understand what exactly I had done.

Then I heard shouting from voices I didn't recognize. Izmir shouted something in Turkish. It sounded like somebody else was on the pool deck with them. I pushed the door open—and my heart fell to my stomach.

SNOT was everywhere.

CHAPTER THIRTY-THREE

THE LAW WON

Plumpy, Gary, and Izmir were in handcuffs. Special Agent Tunley and five other SNOT agents were trying to hold the guys still. Jessica stood next to Tunley, arguing with her, and The Falcon was running in from outside.

I looked again at the tracking dot in my locket.

The Falcon pointed at Tunley. "Get your hands off my team, now."

Tunley held her hand palm out. "Sorry, Coach, it's a Section One Five Emergency, which means I'm the law around here."

The Falcon stepped closer.

"Maybe you didn't hear me, Tunley. You either get your hands off my team, or I'm gonna put *my* hands on *you.*"

Tunley took a small step back and held up a piece of paper. "This is a field warrant for the arrest of these three boys. Turns out they've been the ones pulling all the pranks around Finley this spring."

The Falcon leaned in to look at the warrant, then popped up and studied the guys. "Impossible."

"Just think, Coach," Tunley said, her fingers dancing along Plumpy's arm. "You were with these boys every single day and you didn't pick up on it. One almost thinks you didn't *want* to see it."

Now The Falcon took an uncomfortable step back.

My eyes met Plumpy's. He met me with a blank stare. I needed to do something. I needed to do something *now*.

"Yep, thanks to me, another crisis has been averted. And *these*"—a nauseated look crossed Tunley's face—"these boys are headed to prison for the practice of Ancient Man Activities."

"I still can't believe it," The Falcon said. "They seem weak and harmless to me."

Tunley chuckled. "I assure you, Coach Falcon, that's an easy mistake for a civilian to make. But when you've had the best training SNOT can buy, you see the world through a darker lens. My agents and I just spent the whole day in the woods. You heard me: *the woods*. And guess what we found?"

"Trees?" said The Falcon.

Tunley rolled her eyes like she was dealing with a child. "Evidence, Coach. Evidence proving that it was these boys who were behind those hideous crimes."

The Falcon turned around, looking like she might be sick. Jessica tugged on Special Agent Tunley's arm.

"Aunt Miranda," Jessica said through gritted teeth.

Wait! What?

"You promised. You promised you'd wait until after the synchro meet. We need them to win."

Did she just call her *Aunt?*

Tunley caressed Jessica's cheek. "Sorry darling, my job isn't trophies, it's putting bad guys in prison. And now that I have my evidence, it's time for me to act."

My body was shaking.

"D—did you just call her *Aunt Miranda?*" I stammered.

Jessica rolled her eyes. "Duh, Peter, of course Special Agent Tunley is my aunt."

The Falcon stepped in front of me as I processed this bombshell.

"Well listen, Tunley, my job *is* trophies, and we can't compete tomorrow without these boys. You want to embarrass the entire region because the school hosting the tourney can't field a team?"

"What would you have me do?" Tunley asked.

"You say they're guilty. Fine. But let them compete first, *then* take them away. Heck, after the tournament you can arrest everyone for all I care. But first, we have our synchro meet."

Jessica stepped up. "It won't work. I know these boys. They'll never compete hard if they know they're going to jail."

The Falcon scratched her chin. "Miss Hale's got a point."

Tunley thought about it a moment then raised her finger. "Okay, I'll put them in the local jail tonight. SNOT still needs to go in and search each of their homes. Tomorrow they compete." She cocked an eyebrow and gave the guys a devious smile. "And if Finley doesn't win?" She snapped her fingers. "If Finley doesn't win, I'll make sure a couple years get added to their prison sentence. That should provide them with the proper motivation."

The Falcon brightened up. "Works for me. You don't mind me asking, how'd you tie the evidence to these boys?"

Tunley pointed at me.

"It was our friend Peter here."

Everyone turned and stared.

"Last night, he led my niece to the woods and showed her where his friends have been practicing all their pranks. Thankfully they left a whole bunch of evidence behind."

I wanted to tell the guys it wasn't true, that I didn't mean for any of it to happen. But none of that mattered now.

"Oh, these boys didn't *think* they left evidence behind. I'm sure they thought they were very sneaky the way they tried to clean up their mess." She jabbed a thumb at herself. "But we're better. SNOT could be right under your nose and you'd never suspect it. We collected and analyzed hundreds of different fragments, and it paints a compelling picture of a very dangerous group of boys."

I finally mustered the courage to speak up. "You can't do this," I said.

Tunley tilted her head and walked slowly toward me. "Yes, Peter, I can. I can, and I will."

"But prison? For a bunch of silly pranks?"

"You call them silly? Do you know what would happen to our world if these pranks were allowed to go on? Chaos, Peter. *Chaos.* And life is so much better when there is order."

I turned to Jessica. "Why are you doing this?"

"Peter, Aunt Miranda is right and you know it. All this behavior? It only leads to pain and hardship." She grabbed me by the arm. "And you wouldn't want that, would you?"

"But they're my friends. My best friends."

"Correction, Peter: they *were* your friends. You told me yourself, they abandoned you. Forget about them. Now you have something much better."

I tried to look over at the guys, but Jessica jerked me around to face her. "What?" I asked.

She smiled. "You have me."

The SNOT agents took the guys away. Gary cried, Izmir was stone-faced, and Plumpy looked utterly betrayed.

CHAPTER THIRTY-FOUR

BAD BREATH DRUMMOND

Special Agent Tunley left to search the guys' houses for more evidence, and The Falcon left to prepare for tomorrow's big meet by doing a heavy squat workout. She said the full-body pump was a good way to clear her mind. Jessica stayed with me for a few minutes to tell me to keep my chin up and stay focused for the regional meet. I didn't know whether to yell at her or be happy I wasn't in handcuffs. I had no words. My brain felt numb.

Then I was alone.

My best friends were going to jail, and it was my fault in so many different ways. I'd gotten them into this in the first place. I found the message and the truth. I told them the truth and showed them The Book. I led them to play those pranks. And then I abandoned them for a girl.

A *girl*.

I sat next to the pool for a long time, replaying everything in my mind, trying to figure out how and why it had come to this. But I had no answers.

That's when I heard a familiar creaking. Drummond had pushed his book cart onto the pool deck. He left it there and walked toward me.

"I heard," he grunted.

I said nothing.

"I told you this would happen, Peter. I told you those pranks would get you boys caught."

I wasn't really in the mood for an "I told you so."

"At least you didn't get caught too."

"Yeah, great. I'm the one who got them in trouble, and they're the ones who pay for it."

He waved his hand. "But if you had gotten caught with them, then I'd never be able to get The Book back."

"So you don't even care about what happens to us?"

"Peter, I told you the truth and gave you the book so that you could change things. And I don't see how you can change things sitting in prison." He ran his hand through his hair and twisted his face. "I knew this would happen. Just get me the book before anything else goes wrong."

I shook my head. "It's all about that stupid book with you. I wish I'd never seen that book. I hope I never see it again for the rest of my life."

Drummond scratched the back of his head. "You done feeling sorry for yourself?"

"Excuse me?"

"You need to stop the pity party and pull yourself together. Then I need you to go home and get me that book before it falls into the wrong hands. Got it?"

"Or what?"

"Don't push me, Peter. I gave you your chance and you screwed it up. Now I have to go back to the drawing board and find a new changer."

So it had come to this. I really was going to be left with nothing.

Then something occurred to me. Something that made me angry.

"Or," I said, jumping up, "you could stop being a chicken and start changing things yourself!"

Drummond bent his head low. "What did you just say?"

"I think you heard me, Bad Breath Drummond. You hide away in your dungeon and pretend to tell me and my friends how to change things. But you can't even change your own underwear."

His eyes narrowed and he growled. "I told you to read the book. I told you the book has all the answers. But you refused to read it. All you wanted to do was play a bunch of stupid, foolish pranks." He pointed at me as he came closer. "Don't you dare go blaming this on me. Peter Mills, your friends will spend the next three to five years of their lives in prison because of *your* selfishness. Make sure you never forget that."

I wanted to deck that smelly old man. I wanted to yell at him some more. But I didn't, because deep down, I knew he was right.

This was my fault.

As I watched Drummond push his creaky old book cart out of the pool, something else occurred to me. This was *definitely* my fault, and it was up to me to fix it.

Drummond had told me from the beginning that The Book would have the answers. Well right now, I was in a bad situation. Maybe The Book could help me out. Maybe The Book would have the answer I needed.

There was just one little problem. I didn't have it anymore. Plumpy had The Book. I'd have to go over to his house, get into his room, and get it back.

Then my breath caught. I turned to the exit door and started running.

Because someone else was already heading to Plumpy's house.

Tunley.

CHAPTER THIRTY-FIVE

THE BOOK RESCUE

I approached Plumpy's house from the back. His dad was outside near the driveway, trimming the rosebushes and humming a tune to himself. He was either really glad his son was going to prison or he hadn't heard yet. Which meant Tunley hadn't searched the house, and The Book was probably still there.

I, of course, wouldn't be the one to tell Mr. Booms his son had been arrested. I'd just say that I needed to get something from Plumpy's room. He would understand.

But that's when I saw the flashing lights and heard the sirens. Three SNOT cars were roaring down the road toward the house. I ducked down behind a bush as Mr. Booms stood up and walked toward the cars.

Special Agent Tunley climbed out first.

I was too late.

I crawled away from the house so fast my hands couldn't keep up with the rest of my body and I landed on my face. As I ate a mouthful of wet grass, I realized I couldn't run away. No matter what, Tunley absolutely could *not* get her SNOT-loving hands on that book.

I crawled back to the bush and peeked over it. Mr. Booms was shaking, waving his clippers in the air. Tunley looked like she was either trying to calm him down or was about to slug him. I couldn't tell for sure. But it was clear that using the front door was not an option.

I crawled back behind the bush until I was safely out of sight behind the house, then I sprinted across the back yard to the back patio door. I would slide in, run upstairs, and find The Book. If I had to, I'd flush every page down the toilet. But I couldn't let Tunley find it.

I took a deep breath, put my hand on the door, and pulled.

Locked.

Through the glass patio door, I saw the front door open. I ducked. Mr. Booms entered, followed by Special Agent Tunley.

I was running out of time. I quickly crawled to the side yard, and looked up at Plumpy's bedroom window. He was always saying how he liked to climb out of his second-story window to look at the stars from his roof. Perhaps that meant he left his window unlocked.

My eyes traced down the side of his house. A tall white trellis, covered with green vines, clung to the siding.

I needed that book.

I put my foot on the trellis and felt the skinny wooden lath give a little. This thing was built to hold plants, not a twelve-year-old boy with a bit of squish. I reached up and grabbed another lath of the trellis and slowly, carefully started to climb. With each step upward, it felt like the trellis would snap and I would plummet to the ground. But, incredibly, it held.

I was only a foot below the window and was just reaching up to the ledge above me when the trellis snapped under my foot. I slipped two feet down the trellis before I caught myself. The entire trellis was now shaking, started to loosen from the house. Glancing down, I could see the ground maybe twenty feet below me. If I fell from this height, I'd be sure to break a few bones.

The shaking grew worse, so I threw caution to the wind and scrambled upward. Vines pulled free and laths snapped, but I was able to seize the window ledge just before the trellis completely detached from the wall and fell to the grass below. I was now dangling from a second-story ledge, and my arm and finger strength were the only things preventing me from a big fall and severely broken body.

Thank goodness for synchro. If not for the months of grueling practice, no way would the Squishy of old been able to hang on. But The Falcon and Captain Jessica had prepared me for this moment; I couldn't help but smile at the irony.

I squeezed with my fingertips and pulled my chin up above the ledge.

They weren't in his room yet.

Tunley was taking her time, probably searching the main floor first.

I pushed Plump's large window open, then heaved myself through it, scrambled across the floor, and locked his bedroom door.

Where would Plumpy hide The Book?

There was really only one possibility.

I ripped his covers off his bed and flipped over his mattress. Sure enough, on the underside of his mattress were several strips of duct tape. I tore them off to reveal a rip in the mattress. I put my hand in and felt around inside.

The Book. Thank the Mothers.

I pulled it out and felt the letters carved into the old leather cover. B. A. M.

The doorknob turned and I jumped. A strange voice yelled.

"The boy's door is locked, Special Agent Tunley."

I froze. The doorknob turned again, and this time the door shook.

Shoot.

With the trellis gone, there was no way to climb back out of the window. I was trapped.

"Should I break the door down?" the voice asked.

I needed time. Time to think. To do something.

Plumpy's dresser was next to the door. I went to one side and pushed it in front of the door.

"Wait a second," the voice said. "Is someone in there?"

Now I just needed a way out.

"Special Agent Tunley, you better get up here—someone's in this room!"

I had no choice. I had to jump. Broken bones or not, I needed to take the chance.

There was a pounding at the door.

"Whoever that is, let us in this instant!"

Tunley.

I looked at the trellis, shattered on the ground below. This was going to hurt. A lot. If only I had something to cushion my fall.

A cushion. Like a mattress.

I looked at the mattress. I looked at the window. It was a big window, but not quite big enough for a mattress. But maybe big enough for a folded-up mattress?

It was my only shot.

"We are breaking this door down, do you understand?"

More pounding on the door. Like it was being hit with something. The door shook, and the hinges rattled.

I picked up the mattress, dragged it to the window, and lugged it up onto the sill.

"I can hear you in there!" Tunley shouted.

I shoved the mattress into the window and started to push.

The door was now rattling so hard, the dresser was shaking.

I pushed hard, but the mattress was stuck. I heard a boom behind me and looked back to see that the dresser had moved an inch. Finely manicured fingernails were slipping through a small opening in the door.

"I will get you!" Tunley screamed.

I ran at the mattress and hit it with everything I had. At last it moved, and I kept pushing, picking up momentum as it fell through the window. But I couldn't stop. Before I even knew what was happening, I had tripped and fallen head-first through the window, following the mattress to the ground below.

I screamed, knowing for sure that my squishy twelve-year-old body was about to be permanently embedded in the grass of Plumpy's side yard.

But instead of hitting the ground, I hit the mattress. The impact was still strong enough to knock the wind out of me, but I bounced off without breaking anything and rolled into a bush a few feet away. And there I lay, stuck in the bush and gasping, desperately trying to regain my breath.

When I could finally breathe again, I pulled The Book out of my pants, then worked myself free from the bush and looked to the woods, which were about a hundred yards behind Plumpy's house, across several neighbors' yards. I ran.

I jumped over bushes, hopped fences, sprinted through back yards as fast as I could. When I finally entered the trees I could hear the distant sound of shouting behind me. I kept running.

I zigzagged through the woods, crossed a stream, circled around, and doubled back. Only when I was sure that I was alone and wasn't being followed did I collapse onto a nearby stump and open The Book.

This time I skipped right on past the pranks and went directly to the boring parts. My situation was hopeless, my friends were in trouble, and if there was some way to get them out, I needed to find it fast.

I began to read through The Book as fast as I possibly could. And finally, just when I was getting really discouraged, something caught my eye on the bottom corner of page 179. It was a small entry, and after I read through it, I realized it was not boring. Not boring at all.

I thought it over, read it again, and made a decision.

I could do this. It would be tough, but it just might work.

I stood to leave. My ribs and shoulder both hurt, so I stretched, trying to loosen them up. That's when a piece of paper fell out of the book.

One piece of paper, folded several times. Someone had hidden it in the back of the book. Weird that I'd never come across it before. I unfolded it. It was large, a poster-size document with dashed lines and wording everywhere. Across the top, in large typed letters, it read: "Finley Junior High Swimming Complex."

Building plans.

And written underneath, in Plumpy's handwriting, were the words: "Prank Plan."

So *this* was what the guys had been working on. I spent the next twenty minutes trying to make sense of the plan, and when I finally understood what it was they had been up to, I laughed out loud. It was too bad they wouldn't get a chance to pull that prank. That would sure be something to see.

Hmmm. Of course, *I* wasn't spending the night in jail. And it *would* be an awesome way to end all of this—with the prank to end all pranks. Not to mention a way to pay tribute to the friends I had let down.

I looked at my watch, then scanned Plumpy's plan one last time. I could do this. No, I *had* to do this. Which meant I had one very long night ahead of me.

CHAPTER THIRTY-SIX
PRANK PREPARATION

The prank hinged on an idiotic argument we'd seen Principal Lemming and The Falcon get into earlier that spring, about who had the better fire drill. Lemming wanted what most people would consider a "normal" fire drill: get people off the bleachers and out the doors quickly. But The Falcon called Lemming crazy. She argued that the only reason she'd survived the first fire was because she'd been in the pool the entire time. Therefore, she thought everyone should jump in the pool in the event of a fire, since being immersed in water was naturally the safest place to be. Lemming said that was the dumbest thing she'd ever heard in her entire life. The Falcon then asked if Lemming had ever seen someone in a swimming pool catch on fire. Lemming said she'd never seen *anyone* catch on fire. The argument only went downhill from there.

I was pretty sure the entire conversation had set civilization back a thousand years, but eventually, as with everything, The Falcon got her way. And more importantly, Plumpy got a terrific idea for a prank. Simple yet effective. Set the fire alarm off and watch the entire crowd at the regional synchro meet jump into the swimming pool.

As simple and effective as it was, though, that wasn't enough for Plumpy. No, Plumpy's plan also involved using the school's fire sprinkler system, mixing up invisible ink, releasing red chemicals into the pool, and finding fish.

For most of the plan to succeed, all I needed was a variety of household cleaning chemicals mixed together in just the right way. And fortunately, I knew where to get some fish.

I walked across the hall into my mother's "Me Room." Flute music played on a CD player. The lights were turned down. My mother's black leather chair faced the aquarium.

This was Mom's place to come and relax—although she preferred to call it "dream planning." She came here to get away from Dad and me and to watch those fish. Sometimes I thought she liked those fish better than me.

But now I needed those fish. I filled a trash can with water and scooped the fish into it.

What would I tell my mother when she showed up?

It no longer mattered.

I hauled the unbelievably heavy trash can downstairs and into the garage, and heaved it into the back seat of my dad's car. Then I went into the kitchen and started to grab all the cleaning chemicals I could.

Dad was in the kitchen, cooking. "Peter, what on earth are you doing?"

"What I should have done a long time ago."

"What does that mean?"

"That I haven't been a very good friend."

"And you need all my cleaning products to be a good friend?"

"Yes, I do."

My dad looked like he always did: halfway between terrified and dead. But then finally, something softened a bit and he stood up.

"Fine, take them. But how are you going to carry all that stuff?"

"I was kind of hoping you could drive me."

"I can't. I need to make dinner."

"Dad, it's... really important. You know I don't ever ask you for anything, but right now I really need this. Tomorrow is the last day of finals, and I've got to get this stuff to the guys."

"Why this stuff?"

"Because."

"I'm afraid I'll need something better than 'because,' Peter."

"Because my friends need my help and I can't let them down. Not this time."

My dad stared at me with a curious look on his face. It was a look I'd never seen from him before. I think it might have been... pride.

Finally he grabbed the keys off the counter. He didn't ask any more questions, and ten minutes later he dropped me off in front of the swimming complex. Eddie and the rest of the construction crew were still there, finishing up some last-minute landscaping around the entrance.

"Hey, Peter!" Eddie said as I dragged the heavy trash can along the sidewalk. He looked at me funny. "What's all that stuff for?"

"Lemming gave me detention. Said I had to scrub out the entire swimming complex."

Eddie nodded, then peeked inside the trash can.

"They use fish to clean swimming pools?"

"Surprising, isn't it? I put a little toothpaste on their lips and they leave the pool clean and fluoridated."

Eddie took his hardhat off and ran his hand through his hair. "That's unbelievable."

"Yes, Eddie. Yes it is." I shook my head in disbelief and walked past him with my supplies.

"Hey Peter... I'm sorry to hear about your friends."

I turned. "You heard, huh?"

"We were here when it happened." He grimaced. "That Tunley's bad news."

"You're not a big fan of the special agent?"

He shrugged. "She's scary. Always yelling at me and my guys when she comes around."

"But doesn't The Falcon always yell at you?"

Eddie got a goofy look on his face. "The Falcon's different." Then his expression changed. "I don't like Tunley. Not one bit."

Hmmm. Maybe Eddie could channel that anger. I looked around, trying to come up with an idea. I pictured the prank in my mind and then I looked down at my feet, to the sidewalk where I stood.

"Eddie, how hard would it be to break up this concrete and pour a new sidewalk?"

"Geesh, not that hard, I guess. But why on earth would I do that the day before the big meet?"

"First, you wouldn't do it the day *before* the big meet—you'd do it the day *of* the big meet. And second, you'd do it for a very special reason: because I need your help."

"Really?"

I explained my plan. To my delight, Eddie not only agreed to help, he even added in an improvement of his own.

Then I went inside and started mixing up chemicals according to Plumpy's directions. The kid really was some kind of mad scientist. When I had the batch ready, I took the paintbrush I'd brought and found a ladder in the back room. I set up the ladder against the large white concrete wall across the pool, opposite the huge glass window that led to the outside. I dipped my brush into the batch of chemicals and carefully painted two enormous words. Then I climbed down from the ladder and admired my work.

Perfect. Couldn't see a thing.

Next I mixed up the red dye and sealed it in four zip-lock bags. Plumpy was right: it looked just like blood.

I moved the trash can of fish to the chemical room, found the tank where the chemicals were added every day, and stashed the trash can there. I covered it up with the corner of an old tarp so it wasn't easy to see.

Then I went back to the pool deck and found the light switches. I located the fire sensor nearest to those light switches and taped a lighter underneath.

And finally, and most importantly, I practiced. I practiced turning off the lights, grabbing the lighter, placing it under the fire sensor. I practiced running back to the chemical room where I would be dumping fish into the chemical tanks. I practiced running back to the pool and jumping in. I practiced getting Tunley's attention, jumping out of the pool, and running for dear life until Eddie could execute his part of the plan.

I practiced all of it, over and over again, until I was absolutely sure I was ready. Everything had to be perfect. After all, Tunley deserved my very best shot.

CHAPTER THIRTY-SEVEN

THE REGIONAL MEET

It was late by the time I snuck back into the house. I fell asleep before I hit the bed, and woke what felt like only minutes later to the screaming of a dying cat. At least, that's what it sounded like. When I burst through my door, my dad was standing at the end of the hall.

He wheeled around, one hand running through his hair. "Hey there, Peter." Something pink covered his left cheek. He nodded with his chin toward the Me Room. "Just told your mom the bad news." He was speaking unusually loud, like he wanted Mom to hear. "Was cleaning the fish aquarium yesterday when I accidentally spilled some chemical into the tank. Unfortunately the fish died. Your mother just found out, and obviously she's devastated."

His hair was stuck up in five different directions, his glasses were a bit crooked, and now I realized that the pink thing on his cheek was a handprint. Mom must have decked him good.

But he also wore a curious little smile. He looked…well, for a man who'd just gotten slapped around, he looked strangely alive.

I leaned in to whisper. "How come she didn't notice last night?"

He whispered back. "I saw the fish were gone, so I met her for dinner at a tofu restaurant she's been wanting to try. Told her you were busy studying for exams. By the time we were home, I was rubbing her feet with a new treatment for heavy scabs. She never noticed."

Now it was my turn to be proud. I had no idea my dad had it in him.

"HAROLD!" my mom shouted.

He shrugged and smiled at me. "Duty calls."

"Thanks, Dad."

"Good luck."

"With what?"

"Helping your friends."

It was even harder than usual to concentrate on my exams that day. All I could think about was my plan for the meet, and I couldn't stop worrying over every detail, making sure I was prepared for every contingency.

At last I turned in my last exam and hustled to the locker room to get ready for the meet. When I came out onto the pool deck, the other guys were already there: Tunley and a bunch of SNOTs had apparently brought them to the pool already in their swimsuits. Each one of the guys looked at me like I was the worst person in the world.

Tunley reminded them that if Finley failed to win, their prison sentences would grow... significantly. Then she handed them off to The Falcon and Jessica, who gave our team the final motivational speech of the season.

And then finally, the regional meet began.

We joined the other four schools from our region on the pool deck and paraded in front of the fans. I spotted my parents. Dad gave me a little nod; Mom pointed somewhere and then made that obnoxious face she made when dancing her Me Dance. I looked to where she was pointing and saw Mrs. Hale sitting to her right. On the other side of Mrs. Hale was Special Agent Tunley. The other SNOT agents were sitting below her.

And then I realized something else. We weren't being pelted by dry pasta. The Falcon had said she was going to personally frisk the Noodles fans when they came in, and I guess she followed through. But many of them were actually dressed up in pasta costumes. I had to hand it to them: they took their school, their synchronized swimming, and their whole grains very seriously.

As the coach of the home team, The Falcon determined the order in which the teams would compete; naturally she decided that we would perform our team routine first, to put the pressure on everybody else. As our team of pink flamingos jumped into the pool and moved into position, I glanced up at the crowd and saw Drummond. I could almost smell his odor from the pool—and I was wearing nose plugs.

And then the music started. I shut the rest of my life out, focusing on nothing but the routine. That's a rule of synchro: if you start worrying about what's next, you won't concentrate on the move in front of you. And I definitely didn't know what was going to happen after the meet. All I knew was that I had the next sixty minutes to let synchro be my refuge.

My body took over and I was in the zone. We all were. Our team was performing with what Jessica called PEP: passion, elegance, and perfection. When we were done, the crowd came to their feet, roaring with approval. And when the judges released their scores, we received a perfect ten. Not only that, one of the judges took the unusual step of issuing a statement: "Not just a ten, but the best routine I've seen in years."

Then the other teams performed their routines. The strong Noodles team earned a nine, Franklin scored an eight, Boonthistle also scored a nine and the Crawley team completely lost control of their team and scored a five. The Falcon snickered to Crawley's head coach, "You get a five just for jumping in the pool."

As the other teams performed, I used the time to mentally prepare for the plan. On the other side of the big window, Eddie and his crew were re-pouring one of the sidewalks with fresh cement. *This had better work.*

Next up was the pairs competition. Jessica decided to use the same approach we'd used at our dual meet. That meant her pair would go first, and—as usual—they nailed it. But the rest of the evening didn't go so well for our team, and as the last pairs were about to battle, we had slipped back into a tie for first. And wouldn't you know it: the team we were tied with was Noodles.

And once again, Plumpy and I would be the last pair to go.

As we headed to the pool I whispered to Plumpy, "Hey, I've got a plan for getting you guys out of this, but we have to win this pair, okay?"

He sneered at me. "You have a plan? You going to jump on my back and twist the knife deeper?"

I grabbed his arm and stopped him. "I'm serious, Plumpy. I snuck into your room and got The Book. I found something that can free you guys."

He raised his eyebrows. "What are you saying?"

"No prison."

His eyes opened wide. "You're serious?"

"There's just one catch. We have to win."

His jaw tightened and his lips pursed together. He nodded. "Then let's do this."

We both jumped in the water. Now that the auditorium was packed with fans, I could tell what an impressive building it really was. More than a year since the fire, this awesome-looking structure was not only hosting a regional synchro meet, but Finley Junior High was in position to win for the first time in forever.

Plumpy and I looked over at the pair from Noodles. They smirked at us, and one of them even kissed his bicep then looked up at The Falcon and laughed.

Oh, no he didn't. *Nobody* laughs at The Falcon.

The music started, and we began. And once again, we were *on*. There was no way Plumpy and I were going to lose. But I could see the other pair out of the corner of my eye. And I could tell from the vibe of the crowd: they were on as well. This was going to be close.

We spun. They spun. We jumped and flutter-kicked, they did... whatever they did. I could hear the music coming to the end. *Just hold on,* I thought. We had one sequence of moves left. A sequence Jessica thought we needed for victory.

Plumpy and I started in a back layout, moved perfectly together into a flamingo, moved again into a vertical, and then Plumpy started to sink.

But this time, it was all part of the plan. He came down under me, I bobbed down, and then he burst out of the water and threw me high into the air. As I rocketed upward, I did a 360-degree spin with my leg held perfectly straight against the side of my head. I even kept my toe pointed straight like The Falcon taught me.

When the music stopped, the crowd exploded. I even heard a few bravos. I didn't know if we had done enough to win, but the crowd knew that this was the way synchro *should* be. Sure, our pairs weren't as talented as Jessica's and a few others. But we were the last, our teams were vying for the championship, and we'd left everything out in the pool.

The Noodles pair came over. One guy shook my hand. The other guy shook Plumpy's hand and said, "May the best team win."

Plumpy raised his finger in the air. "Don't worry. We did."

CHAPTER THIRTY-EIGHT

TWO BEAUTIFUL WORDS

We joined our team on the pool deck while the judges consulted for the next few minutes. Tunley and the SNOT agents had descended the bleachers and now stood on the pool deck too, waiting. Jessica made us all join hands in a show of team solidarity. The Falcon kissed both of her biceps for good luck, then growled at a little kid in the first row.

The lead judge stepped up to the microphone. "A brilliant competition tonight, a tribute to the high level of synchronized swimming in our region. It was incredibly close, with the top two teams battling it out to the very end. But..." She turned to a member of the band, and a drum roll started. "...in the end, the winning team... of tonight's Regional Championship... is... for the first time in fifteen years...

"Finley Junior High!"

The crowd went nuts and our team jumped up and down like maniacs. The Falcon ran along the pool deck, beating her chest and pumping her fists. She even ripped both sleeves off of her shirt, revealing two enormous biceps with new tattoos that dwarfed her Harry and Sally tattoos. Emblazoned with hot pink ink, the left bicep now said *BITE*, and the other bicep now said *NOODLES*.

I never said The Falcon was the classiest person in the world, but I was glad she was my coach.

But the fun was just beginning. While my team and the crowd continued to go crazy, I took advantage of all the chaos to quietly slip away. I sidled up next to the light switches. Took one last breath, counted to three, and then hit the lights and grabbed the lighter in one motion.

When the lights went out, the crowd panicked and screamed. I ran ten feet to the nearest fire sensor and put the lighter directly under it. Five seconds later, the fire alarm sounded and the overhead fire sprinklers activated. By now the emergency lights had kicked in, and gave me enough light to see by as I ran to the chemical room and dumped the trash can of fish into the chemical tank, then opened the valve to release them into the pool.

I raced back to the pool deck, where The Falcon was now at the base of the bleachers, grabbing fans and heaving them into the pool left and right, yelling at everybody to "Jump in the pool or die a fiery death!" I grabbed the stickpin I'd stuck in my swim cap and jumped into the pool as well.

The good thing about a one-piece swimsuit—maybe the *only* good thing—was it made hiding things in my belly super easy. I drove the pin into my squishy belly four different times, and red dye started to leak from the dye packs I'd hidden there. At just about the same time, the people in the water started noticing the tiny little fish swimming around them. I swam underwater, weaving through the maze of people, doing my best to spread the fake blood.

Who would have thought that a few goldfish and a little fake blood could be made to look like an out-of-control attack by vicious, swarming piranha? Good old Plumpy.

The effect was immediate. Screams echoed through the swimming complex and The Falcon could no longer keep people in the pool. They climbed out en masse and raced for the nearest door. Unfortunately, it was locked.

Good old Eddie.

The crowd turned and raced for the other exit, at the other end of the pool deck. Eddie opened the door to let them out, and they charged across the plywood sheet that lay over the freshly poured concrete.

Time for the final piece of the prank. I searched the chaos for Special Agent Tunley. There—she was standing on the pool deck, scanning the crowd, no doubt looking for the perpetrators of these Man Activities. I made sure to catch her eye, and then I channeled every bit of The Falcon I could muster and gave her the double biceps kiss.

I was marking my territory. And little did she know, Miranda Tunley, the biggest SNOT of them all, was about to become my territory.

I swam right for her, weaving between the people still clambering to get out of the pool.

"Hi, Miranda!" I yelled.

Her eyes settled on my face and her expression turned sour as she dropped into attack position.

"The name's Special Agent Tunley," she growled.

I laughed at her. Laughed right in her face. "You'll never catch me, Miranda."

She squinted, snorted, and dove.

I was already five yards away when she entered the water. Months of synchro training had made me quick as a cat hit by lightning. She chased me to the other end of the pool. I merely zigzagged around her, circled back, and climbed out. By now the other SNOTs had hauled everyone else out of the pool. It was just me and Tunley now.

"Oh, Miranda!" I waved as she swam furiously to the edge.

She slapped through the water like a maniac, grabbed the ledge, and climbed out with a primal scream. Her white SNOT uniform was dyed red from the water.

I would never be able to outrace a well-trained SNOT on foot. At least not for very far. Luckily, I only needed to make it to the door. The far exit, to be precise.

I sprinted to the door, pushed it open, and leaped at an angle to clear the wet cement—the wet cement that was no longer covered with plywood. Got to hand it to Eddie—he'd done everything I'd asked and then some. I heard Miranda yelling behind me, so I ran a few more steps, then hit the ground and rolled.

I looked back just in time to see the most beautiful sight in the world.

Special Agent Tunley burst through the door at full speed, saw the cement at the last moment, leapt into the air, and started waving her arms like a bird learning to fly. But apparently SNOT training didn't involve flight lessons.

With the splat heard round the world, she fell face first into the freshly poured cement.

What happened next was all because of the particular genius of an otherwise dumb guy. Eddie said that if we really wanted to get Tunley, he should dig the sidewalk really deep and pour three or four feet of cement.

And so it was with great joy that I watched Special Agent Miranda Tunley not just land in the cement, but *sink* into it. When she realized what was happening, she lifted her face out of the grey sludge just far enough to manage a muffled scream. The other SNOT agents came over to help her, but pulling someone out of concrete is not such an easy thing to do. As Tunley flailed around, they fell in too. Tunley then yelled for Jessica to help—and Jessica fell into the cement as well.

That was a nice little bonus I hadn't expected.

Finally, The Falcon came to the rescue. She pushed her way through the crowd and lifted each one of them out of the cement as easily as if she were pulling ice cubes out of water. She pulled Tunley out last, and I do believe she let the special agent squirm a bit first.

I was on my feet now, slowly moving away from Tunley, when I noticed the crowd directing their attention back toward the swimming complex. Noses were pressed up against the glass, and all eyes were fixed on the big white concrete wall on the other side of the pool.

Two gigantic words mysteriously appeared on that wall. This, of course, was all the genius of my oldest and best friend. Plumpy had found a section in The Book about creating invisible ink. Apparently, invisible ink usually operates by using an agent and a reagent. The agent is what you use to write your invisible message, and the reagent is what you use to cause the invisible ink to be made visible. Plumpy had spent some time experimenting to find out what kind of chemical would react with the flame retardant that came out of the fire sprinklers, and then developed an invisible ink based on that chemical. And that's precisely what I'd used to paint on the walls. So when the chemical from the fire sprinklers hit the wall, the invisible ink became visible. And now, after a few minutes, the two words were unmistakable.

Two words; a simple message. Two words summing up what us boys had always felt about the world in which we lived. Two beautiful words:

GIRLS STINK

CHAPTER THIRTY-NINE

A REAL MAN

After Eddie was kind enough to hose off Tunley, Jessica, and the SNOT agents, Tunley looked around like a crazy woman. I knew exactly who she was looking for.

And I wasn't going anywhere.

"Oh Miranda," I called out cheerily, smiling and waving. She shook herself like a dog, wiped more cement off of her face with her wet sleeve, and marched toward me. Her SNOT agents had by now regained control of the guys.

"Did I get your attention?" I asked as she stopped ten feet from me.

"This was *you*?" she spat through cement-covered teeth.

"Yes, Miranda, it was."

Jessica came up alongside her aunt. Half her face was still covered in concrete. Her hair was matted down. She looked like a strange, deformed statue of Helga McMasters. She pointed at me. "*You* did this?"

"Oh, hi there, Sweetie." I motioned toward her face. "This is a really good look you've got going. How could I describe it? Oh, I remember. Ugly makeup. But don't worry, you do ugly just fine."

Jessica's confused and bewildered expression instantly turned to white-hot anger, and she snarled at me. There she was: the girl I hadn't seen for the last month. Good old Jessica. The Ice Princess was back, and she was either foaming at the mouth or the concrete was reacting in a strange way with her saliva.

"*I. Will. Kill. You.*"

Ha, the joke was on her. I didn't care. But apparently somebody did.

Tunley put a hand on Jessica's shoulder and held her niece back. Then Tunley turned to me. "So you're saying that you singlehandedly pulled this prank tonight?"

"No, Special Agent Dumbly, I'm saying that I singlehandedly pulled *all* the pranks this year."

"Impossible."

"Maybe for a girl."

"Watch it, Mr. Mills."

"I'm serious, Dumbly. Look at the three morons you've arrested for my pranks." I pointed at the guys. I could tell by the confusion on Plumpy's face that he still didn't fully understand what I was doing.

Tunley folded her arms and lifted one of her eyebrows. "It's Tunley."

"Huh. Why do I keep thinking 'Dumbly'?" I smiled sweetly. "Anyways, do you know how much time and work went in to playing all of those pranks? And then to have you come along and arrest these fools for doing them? I'm not going to let you give *them* credit for *my* work."

"I was under the impression these 'fools' were your friends."

I laughed. "They're better than girls, if that's what you mean, but friends? I don't think so. These guys couldn't find their way out of a paper bag with a flashlight. I wouldn't exactly call them friend material."

"So you're saying all that stuff I found in the clearing…"

"It was mine. That's what I'm saying."

Plumpy stepped forward, but a SNOT agent pulled him back. "Don't do this, Peter."

I waved my hand at him. "Shut up, Leonard. You've been leeching off my superior brainpower for far too long. And you will not, I repeat, *not* screw this up for me."

I stared at him, trying some of that super-silent communication I had used with Bernie.

Tunley stepped closer. "You do realize the three years I offered these morons yesterday was *before* the prank you just pulled. It's off the table now."

I shrugged. "Who cares? Any place is better than Finley Junior High."

"I don't think I'll have any trouble convincing the judge that fifteen to twenty years makes more sense for you."

I swallowed hard. "Twenty?"

"Oh yeah, twenty years in a *prison*." She watched me take it all in. "Just so we're clear, it's your story that you pulled *all* of these pranks?"

I thought about The Book, about the section I'd read last night in the woods. About how to be a real man. It was the only way I could save my friends.

"Believe me, it's not a story. You're telling me I get the privilege of being in a prison for the next twenty years of my life? I'll take that deal any day."

Jessica stepped forward. "I thought you were smarter than this, Peter."

"And I thought you had evolved into a fully formed human being over the last month. Seems like we were both wrong."

Tunley stepped in front of her niece, pulled a pair of handcuffs out of her soggy back pocket, and motioned for me to spin around. I did, and she slapped those cold metal cuffs around my wrists, then yanked hard on my arms.

"Believe me, darling, this will be twenty years you will not enjoy."

"Are you going to be in prison with me?" I asked.

"Of course not," she sneered.

"Then I'll enjoy it just fine."

I was staring at my friends now. The SNOT agents were removing their cuffs. The guys walked toward me.

Gary's lip was quivering. "Don't, Peter," he said.

Izmir was stone-faced. Then he shook his head. "Not right."

Plumpy's eyes were wet. His hands were in his pockets. "We can't let you do this."

"Like I said, Plumps, you guys are nice enough, but I pulled those pranks and there's nothing you can do to steal credit for them. So just stop trying."

"More of that gentleman nonsense?"

I shrugged. "Maybe."

Plumpy bit his lip and shook his head. "I guess you're not so squishy after all."

"Thanks, I've been working on it."

Plumpy dropped his head down and backed away.

"And Plumpy." His head snapped up; he was looking right at me.

"Yeah, Peter?"

"I'm sorry about—"

He cut me off with a shake of his head. "Me too."

Tunley dragged me across the parking lot to her SNOT car. I turned and took one last look at what was left of my life. Jessica was shaking her head like she wanted to kill me. My mother looked like she was throwing up in a nearby bush. My dad, though? He stood straighter and taller than I'd ever seen him in my life, watching from afar. I offered him a smile, but I'm not sure he could see it.

We were just about to get in the car when I smelled something hideous. Sure enough, Bad Breath Drummond was limping in our direction.

"Peter," Drummond coughed. Tunley retreated from a blast of his toxic odor. Maybe Drummond was here to save me with his lethal weapon breath.

"What about BAM?" he asked.

Of course. The only thing Drummond cared about was The Book. I sighed. "Talk to Plumpy."

Tunley gave me a curious look. "Bam? What is that, some kind of a code word?"

"As a matter of fact, it is," I replied. "Stands for 'Buttons and Mints.' Drummond here was going to help us with the decorations for our buttons-and-mints themed quilting party."

Tunley shook her head in disgust and looked up to the sky. "Thank the Mothers I'm not a boy." Then she shoved me in the back of her car and locked the doors.

As Tunley pulled the car away, I turned around for one last look. My friends were running after the car. Izmir ran faster than the others, then stopped, thrust his chin into the air, balled up his fists, and yelled something into the night. And even from inside the car, I knew exactly what he was saying.

"Ottoman Turkish Empire!"

He kept yelling it over and over. I looked back until I could no longer see his face. Now *my* eyes were wet.

I was gonna miss him too.

EPILOGUE

Four weeks after Peter was sent to prison, the doorbell rang at Plumpy's house. A delivery man stood at the doorway, a yellow envelope in his hands.

"Letter for Plumpy Booms."

Plumpy took the letter and read it. A short note, scribbled in familiar handwriting:

Clearing. Package. Now.

Plumpy's heart leapt.

Thirty minutes later, Plumpy, Gary, and Izmir made their way into the clearing. Sitting on the ground, in between three fallen logs, was a white cardboard box. They ran to the box and ripped it open. Inside, a pink envelope lay on top of another box. Plumpy opened the letter and read it aloud.

> *Hey guys! Prison is awesome. Okay, awesome's a little strong. But it's better than you think. I get to hang around a*

bunch of cool guys all day, and I've learned more about being a man than you can possibly imagine.

Be sure to read The Book. All of it. The time will come for us boys to rise up. And when that happens, you better be ready. And one way to do that is to make sure you're eating right.

That's why I've included the other box. Don't worry. It's not possum, but it's amazing the kinds of things you can get your hands on while in a prison.

I miss you guys like crazy. Long live the Beef Jerky Gang!

Your pal,

Peter

Izmir opened the second box. Inside, ice cubes were melting around a white Styrofoam container. Gary opened the lid—and revealed something none of them had ever seen before in their lives.

Reddish-brown color. Marbled textured. Slightly funky smell. They'd never seen it before, but they knew exactly what it was.

Beef.

That day in the woods, Plumpy, Gary, and Izmir prepared and cooked up their first batch of beef jerky. And that night, as they thought about their good friend Peter, they ate their first chunks of salty, chewy goodness.

And while Gary and Izmir worked on a new prank they'd just learned, Plumpy looked up above the trees to the stars of the night and wished his friend Peter could hear him. He imagined that Peter would ask him how the jerky tasted, and Plumpy knew exactly how he would respond.

"Peter, the beef jerky wasn't as good as we thought it would be."

Plumpy put his finger in the air.

"It was better."

Then he returned to the note and read the last part again.

P.S. Plumpy, you'll never guess who visited me the other day. She told me that in order for Finley to win the National Synchro Tournament next fall, she's going to need me on the team. And apparently, she's got a plan.

THE END

Just Finished Reading The Beef Jerky Gang?

Here's what you should do next

1. Throw Away All the Salad in Your House
2. Make Beef Jerky
3. Eat Beef Jerky
4. Create Gigantic Fart Noises
5. Give The Book To Somebody Else

    Seriously, give it away. In order to change the world, you can't hold on to a book. Be a changer, not a keeper. Use this handy dandy chart to help you out. Write down your name, your home town, the date you finished the book, and the date you passed it on. And no matter what happens, remember, Buttons And Mints!

YOUR FIRST NAME	YOUR HOME TOWN	DATE YOU FINISHED THE BOOK	DATE YOU PASSED THE BOOK ON

ABOUT THE AUTHOR

Daniel Kenney and his wife Teresa live in Omaha, Nebraska with zero cats, zero dogs, one gecko, and lots of kids. When those kids aren't driving him nuts, Daniel is busy writing books, cheering on the Benedictine Ravens, and competing in the annual World's Strongest Dan Competition. Find out more at www.danielkenney.com.

Made in the USA
Middletown, DE
07 February 2015